I0763390

Lawrence Johns

Golf Strategy

An Essay On Golf In The New Medieval

First Limited Burgess Society Hardback Edition

First 300 numbered copies signed and dated by the Author are available exclusively from the publisher at consciouspublishing.com

For my father

Robert Johns

Golf Strategy

Acknowledgements:

Illustrations from the Codex Manesse used with kind permission of the University of Heidleburg, Germany

Reproductions of Alan Sorrell paintings used by kind permission of Julia Sorrell.

The stanza on Page 5 is from the prologue to Canterbury Tales by Geoffrey Chaucer.

The photo of Lawrence Johns is by Clarence Johns.

Book & Cover Design - Minerva Designs

ISBN: 978-1-929096-10-7

Conscious Publishing

2034 SW Vermont Street
Portland, OR 97219
consciouspublishing.com

Books by Lawrence Johns

Philosophy

Sensazioni

The Individual

Poetry

Love And Hate

Beyond Exile

Golf Strategy

Golf is the greatest game. It fascinates the mind. It challenges the body. It ravishes the deeper emotions. The true golfer is a lover. He only feels totally present in the presence of his beloved. He lives for that rare and transcendent round when woods, irons and putter flow into a joyous union of intent. The true golfer is a lover and a fool---a deluded, jealous, precarious fool who'll hazard everything to shine brighter in the sweet rays of his beloved's affection. After one bad shot he's immediately avalanched with doubt, stabbed by a thousand daggers of recrimination, desperate beyond words and often beyond reason. He instantly loses his being-here. He's suddenly no-where, looking for a rope, a book, a quick fix.

Golf is the greatest game, but a lover only listens to advice from a distant source. This book comes from that distance. It arrives with the admission that much of what you know about golf is shaped by the urgency to have your love for the game reciprocated. If one day you happen to go low, the anguish and frustration of a hundred rounds is quickly forgiven. On a wretched day a bad swing or a bad bounce is all it takes to fall into the dark vortex of a lover's depression, where every shot is a crescendo of panic and exhilaration leading to the inevitable self-destruction of the wishful thinker. To win at golf you must elevate your will, control your emotions and destroy all evidence of self-delusion.

A Knight ther was, and that a worthy man,
That from the tyme that he first bigan
To ryden out, he lovede chyvalrye,
Trouthe and honour, fredom and curteisie.

The lover isn't a state of mind you can slip off like a tattered jacket once you grasp strategy. As a passionate golfer you'll always be a lover and fool---this is the nature and beauty of passion. The difference is that you'll be a *knowing* lover. While your fellow competitors are riding an emotional roller coaster in the steel cage of uncertainty you'll always know what to do with the shot at hand. Golf knowledge is the first prerequisite to golf freedom. A hooked drive into the trees, a seven-iron approach that settles to the center of the green, or a tricky downhill putt for birdie all create unique conditions of being-here. A fresh set of psychological and athletic problems for the golfer to solve. Each hole is a personal event that profoundly influences the next event and a fair test of your evolving freedom.

Golf strategy optimizes your play on each hole based on how you played the last. It frontloads your thinking so you don't doubt or second guess yourself during tournament play. It deletes your self-defeating emotions so every competitive round is a manifestation of your personal will. And it presumes a strong intent to win. If you feel some resistance to strategy it's likely you've come to identify playing competitive golf with fighting a stubborn and shifting set of internal demons. If you're habituated to the drama of watching a positive image of yourself battle a negative under the merciless sun of irrational expectations you have a thousand reasons to deny or turn a blind eye to strategy. Any philosophy of winning would spoil the intrigue, the unpredictable thrill of this all-too-human struggle.

You may prefer to leave it to fate, to chance. You may even come to agree with the decadents who claim losing is more coherent, more satisfying to the modern spirit. When winning proves too demanding, losing offers the magnificent illusion of control---you can arrive at your station any time you wish. So it's never too early to ask the right questions. Do you truly want to know? To win? To be free? Or do you prefer playing *at* golf?

It can take a second, it can take a lifetime but once you see yourself as the lover you must discard this truth for one more powerful. The battlefields of love are marshaled by absurdity, madness and random ecstasies. The smallest mistaken gesture, the meanest unspoken word brings the castle down. Nothing is ever under control, nothing is ever as it seems. Love games are distinguished by their overabundance of cruelty, tenderness, and confusion. Millions of social golfers worldwide accept this romantic madness as sufficient compensation for their psychological and financial investments in the game. It's also why they cheat. Love's a game naturally, most efficiently played *outside the rules.* All's fair. Cheating works. The more brazen the better. There's no logic, no rules, no strategy to love beyond the classic motto that *fortune favors the bold.*

As you read this, ten thousand golfers are trying to seduce the game with a fairway wood over long water or a chip-in from deep greenside rough. In fantasy they're Tiger Woods. In reality they'll botch the shot and cheat somewhere on the back nine for compensation and decompression. They're lost to the cruelty and confusion of it all, lost to the upstream hope of experiencing golf ecstasy once again. All's fair. No rules. Golf by lovers is all about grand gestures and complex personal delusions.

Competitive golf rises above seduction and must respect the rules inherited from ancient golf tradition. Without universally accepted rules no victory can be historically acknowledged or celebrated. Gary Player had his illustrious image permanently tarnished by the hint of a suspicion he was tamping down grass behind his ball. Ask Colin Montgomerie about Jakarta. The perennial philosophy of the game is embodied in its conservative, self-regulating rules, so a successful strategy based on the rules necessarily *favors the cautious.* Golf shots aren't love letters. Cheating *never* works. To win at tournament golf you must cease to be a daring, shameless lover. You must will to will more. You must be a hunter, a warrior---a knight.

The knight symbolizes confidence and intelligence. His honor requires consistent submission to the rules. His self-discipline repudiates the all-too-common modern luxuries of self-contempt and material vanity. He's constantly meditating on his will and doesn't allow idle conjectures or counterproductive truths to remain bubbling long in consciousness. His will must take on reality. The tournament must be won. If for one instant he fears another knight is stronger, if for one heartbeat he doubts his position at the top, he's already lost. Chess grandmasters, living in a computer-controlled henhouse of ELO numbers, must hypnotize themselves into believing they can win a tournament against higher-rated opposition just to finish in their predicted place. Without this confidence they'd lose every game---including the ones against lower-rated opponents.

Chris Moneypenny won The World Series of Poker after qualifying online in a $40 satellite tournament. The irrepressible focus of a tyro overwhelmed the nonchalance and celebrity glitter of the top professional poker players in the world. Confidence gets the player to the final table, intelligence wins the final pot. Total battle awareness is essential to the knight's will to power. He senses subtle changes in the battlefield, in the shifting phases of the game. He's always alert for the occasion to call a penalty on himself when no witness can see the infraction. It makes him exponentially stronger. It publicly proclaims his superiority, his higher duty.

During the 1925 US Open at Worchester Country Club Bobby Jones called a penalty on himself when his ball imperceptibly moved in the rough. This one stroke cost him an outright win. When such pride of purpose results in the loss of a major tournament the knight becomes *invincible.* In 1926 Bobby won the US Open and the British Open, and in 1930 he cashed his Worchester marker by winning golf's first Grand Slam---the US Open, the US Amateur, the British Open and the British Amateur.

The knight is a contradiction mounted on a riddle, his honor the true killer instinct.

A Quick History Of How We Got Here. Scottish knights and aristocrats were playing golf in the 1300s and our first written record of golf is in 1457, when King James II banned the game because it distracted his soldiers from critical archery practice. This tension between military priorities and golfing pleasure continued for two generations until King James IV lifted the ban in 1502 and persuaded his royal bow maker to make up a complete set of clubs. In 1552 Mary Queen of Scots was the first woman to play golf in Scotland and was severely admonished in 1567 for audaciously golfing a few days after the murder of her husband. Golf was born when knighthood was in flower and has carried much of this chivalric imprinting forward. The bloom faded as the individual valor of armored knights on the battlefield was made increasingly irrelevant - first by the longbow and then by the introduction of guns and cannons into 17th Century warfare.

For the next two hundred years golf was the ward of Scottish Freemasons, a sporting pretext for banquets and secret ceremonies. After the Reverend Adam Paterson's invention of the gutty ball in 1848 golf was taken up by sportsmen of all classes and by the end of the 19th Century Scottish golf pros had transformed domestic poverty into global passion for the noble game. American Golf was born in a humble apple orchard in Yonkers on November 14, 1888. From a thick cloud of obscure paternity claims John Reid is now casually accepted as her father.

By 1900 America had over a thousand golf courses. Boosted by televised tournaments in the 1960s American Golf experienced exponential growth in rounds played, PGA tournament purses, and corporate sponsorship. Quite willingly, she became the glowing bride of American big business and her seasonal consort was the corporation that most coveted the disposable income of her healthy demographic. She became a vast commercial zone of equipment manufacturers, resort and real estate communities, sportswear, books, instructional videos, and golf-themed gifts for every holiday on the calendar.

Today this fertile marriage is under intense pressure. American Golf is experiencing her first economic contraction. Corporations are folding up their supplier party tents and flapping into the sunset. The number of rounds played is down. Equipment sales are down. More importantly, the latest American generation shows remarkably little interest in playing or following the game. They prefer video games and fitness training, bicycles and ultimate fighting. So how will golf survive? It's survived gunpowder, the hydrogen bomb, and Lady Gaga. It's survived the French, Russian and Chinese political revolutions. It's transcended the volcanic social eruptions triggered by the Industrial Revolution and the internet. No matter how dramatically the form and function of Western Civilization changes, golf survives by staying true to its ethical philosophy. *In this sense golf is decidedly more real than history.*

B
A

A Quick Note On The Importance Of This Book. Golf books started appearing 150 years ago and today we have an immense library of golf information and entertainment. Amazon.com currently lists over 180,000 golf titles in print and there are millions of golf books passionately kept for reference in private collections and proudly displayed on the coffee tables of America. You know these books. You haven't read them all, but you know these books. They range from obtuse dissertations on the muscles used in the golf swing to racy stories about barnstorming the PGA Tour in the 40s and 50s. One salient fact you may have missed is that *they were all written by lovers.*

These books contain millions of photographs extolling the exquisite beauty of golf courses around the world, millions of tips and swing techniques, millions of amusing anecdotes taken from the historical sweep of golf, but they're not *serious.* They're a kind of *golf erotica,* they bank on the voyeuristic desire *to make crazy love to golf* like the wealthy members of famous clubs, like the celebrity touring pros. These millions of golf books lack depth, method, or theory. Most importantly, they all *lack strategy.* You hold in your hands the first serious work on golf strategy, the first to propose a *theoretical method* for winning golf tournaments.

This book is written for you knights among the touring pros, you knights among the club pros, you knights among the competitive amateurs, and with great respect for you knights among the weekend warriors---those of you who work two or three jobs and still have the fire in the belly that asks on the first tee, “What’s the bet?” That’s the beauty of theory. *For a golf strategy to be considered valid for any pro it must be verifiable by every amateur.*

Analyzing this vast golf bibliography one could rightfully inquire, “Why did it take 150 years to invent golf game theory?” I don’t know. Nor do I know why it took me this long to fine-tune feedback from my students, understand the power of the cultural phase-shift, and fight through 40 drafts. This book is a highland blend of golf ideas, and it’s taken over 15 years in the barrel to distill them correctly. In the New Medieval every accelerating dawn is heavily radiated by high strangeness, faith-based ferocity and institutional lunacy. In this time of omniscient superstition and efficient media conditioning new golf knowledge must begin with a firm stroke of *the serious.*

Golf is the greatest game, so naturally it's dominated to the quick by the lesser games of war, religion, politics, economics and culture. Because the touring pro must constantly subjugate his deepest and most fragile feelings to the combat state in order to transform the unrelenting pressures of competition into victory he's particularly susceptible to the emotional fallout of divorce, breakups and betrayals. If his wife isn't a lady he's simply undone. Nobody can make a crucial six-footer if he thinks his wife is sleeping with her lawyer. While it may only start as a whisper in the locker room, heartbreak is the primary cause of career shipwreck on the PGA and LPGA Tours.

Winning golf requires total emotional serenity. If you truly want to win tournaments you must first do this---turn to your lady and ask her infinite help. If her answers are evasive or equivocal you can stop reading now---every word that follows will be white noise, signifying nothing and inspiring less. If her answers are sincere and supportive, immediately start building a strong castle together *so it can withstand the inevitable assaults of malice and misfortune to come.*

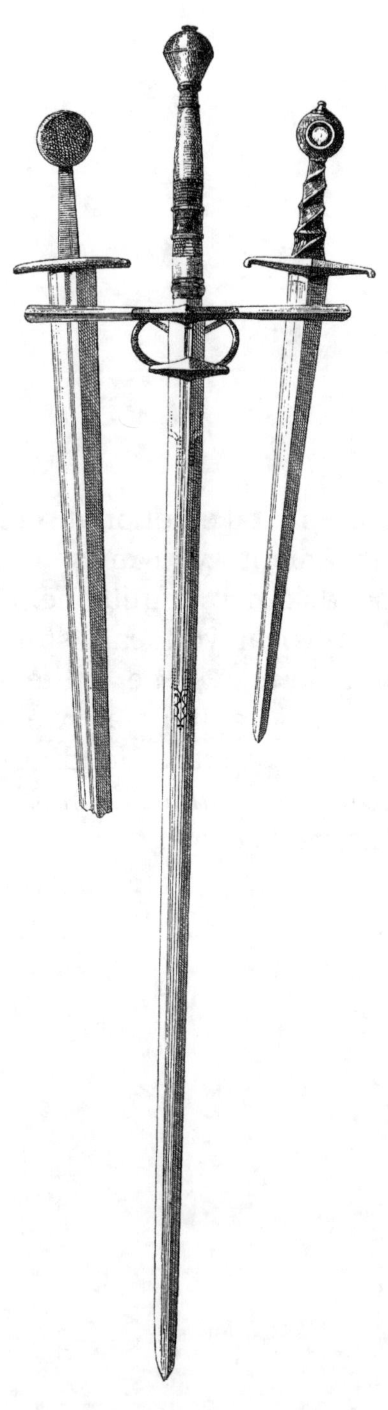

The Johns Golf Strategy

1. Play the first 3 holes for par.

2. Play the next 14 holes for par until:

    a) You make birdie or better; then play for birdie until you make bogey or worse then play for par.

    b) You make bogey or worse; then play for par until you make birdie or better then play for birdie.

    c) You are 5 over par; then play in for birdie.

3. Play the last hole for par unless you need birdie to win.

Sportsmen will notice that the key concept of my strategic system is momentum. One of the required instincts of an NBA coach is to recognize and immediately act upon shifts in game momentum. To win a pro basketball contest he needs to call reliable plays for his hot shooters, bench the cold, and call time-outs when he can best subvert the positive momentum of the opposing team. Momentum theory is also critical in casino blackjack, where you increase or decrease the size of your bet depending on what cards have been most recently exposed. Great comebacks in college and pro football all hinge on big momentum swings in the second half of the game. Another sharp analogy is poker, where theory shows the pro player how control of momentum creates bigger pots when you have the winning cards and greater opportunities to win with bluffs when you have blanks.

In golf the optimum winning strategy is aggression after a good hole and caution after a bad one. You can cut the corner with your drive, approach a tucked pin, and try to drain the putt from any distance after a birdie, but aim for the middle of the fairway, the center of the green, and lag your putt after a bogey. One advantage of this performance-based momentum system is that it minimizes ego override. The ego wants it all back in one rip. The ego can't endure failure for more than a few seconds. Las Vegas was built on this all-too-human fallacy and it feeds 24/7 on the flesh of players who allow a single negative event to snowball into a life of pain and resentment.

Never double up after a bad shot or a bad hole. It's *the* sucker play. Be cautious. Play the J. A fool may feel his manhood threatened after chunking a shot into the lake, but the knight *has nothing to prove to anybody*. He never brings the value of his being-here into question. His confidence is absolute, new threats *stimulate* his intelligence. His immediate goal is par. He doesn't roll the dice for a miracle. He's cool. His ego is lashed to the mast. A bogey just makes things a little more interesting. After a birdie he automatically goes into attack mode and things get *extremely* interesting.

Play for par. It sounds simple, commonsensical, but understanding its supreme strategic value requires a revaluation of many common golf perspectives. Consider the First Rule. In the theory of classic course design the first three holes are considered starters, warm-ups, presenting clear and minor obstacles to the player. It's acknowledged that one has just arrived by cab, car or plane, been summarily introduced to the putting green and driving range by a taciturn gap-toothed caddy and can't be expected to get the kinks out of his back until three greens have gone by. It's admitted that it takes some time to get into the flow of the game, and that the sting of early errors can poison a magnificent golfing day.

This traditional view remains valid today even if contemporary designers have been induced to introduce dragons into the landscape from the very first tee and you rarely use a caddy. Magazine rankings are a career concern for golf architects, and it's virtually impossible to design a national top-ten track---with all its attendent publicity and real estate value---beginning with three easy starters. Because many modern championship courses begin with three monsters to accommodate commercial interests the amateur competitor can jump his rails quite early, hacking through the last fifteen holes in a numb vacuum state on the way to the bar.

The touring pro can ill afford to start behind the eight-ball, and should never underestimate the importance of this First Rule. You've just arrived by cab, car or plane and can't be expected to get the kinks out of your back until three greens have gone by. The physical transition from driving and eating to playing winning golf on a championship course takes about an hour, so don't force things---it takes time for the mind, the large muscle groups, and the small muscle groups to renew their acquaintance. Play the first three holes with a studied wariness, a simple reverence and they will return the favor by setting up the rest of the round.

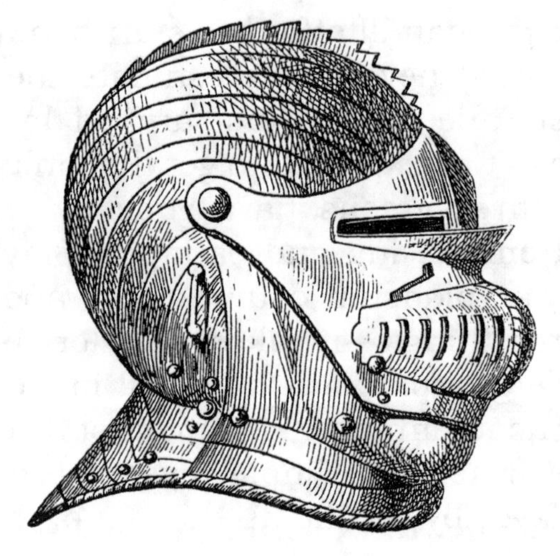

The paradox of warrior consciousness is knowing what you have to do and *also* knowing you have to stay unaware of this knowing. This conflux of awareness and unawareness takes total concentration. The primary cause of failure in all games and sports is the destructive influence of the observing self. To win golf tournaments you need to gear your self-awareness way down, gear your world-awareness way up and let your body *play.* This is no easy trick for players with highly developed imaginations zipping forwards and backwards in time. You can see yourself eating Porterhouse after posting your winning score, you're replaying a yanked four-footer in a mental loop for weeks, months, years. One bad hole early in your golf career can dominate your life perspective like an intestinal parasite.

To keep yourself in the present you have to make everything conscious unconscious and everything metaphysical physical. Your rational strategy creates your physical strength. Playing means you know what you're doing *without observing yourself knowing or doing it.* Play happens when your tournament experience, ball striking skills, and personal psychology become instinctive movement---a dance, a sequence of martial art forms. You know your chosen shot will come off because *you already enjoy the physical pleasure of your hands on the grip.*

The concentration of winning golf is the total focus of a child playing with his toy. The knight *is* the child. The knight *is* the world. Only when you *are* the environment can you adapt the shot to changing conditions. Only when you *are* the environment can you will the win. If you're watching, teaching or judging yourself over the ball you're playing *at* golf. The shot won't come off because the intellectual impulse to control things shuts everything down. A playing child is oblivious to outside observers. He's also unaware of observing himself---he's just *being here*, bccausc for him play *always means life-or-death.*

So now that you're careful with the first three holes and can trust your body over the ball, let's examine *par.* Hugh Rotherham of the Coventry Club in England invented the concept in 1890. He worked out what a "perfect golfer" would score on his club's Whitely Common course and called it the "ground score". This term was quickly replaced throughout the British Isles by a snatch from a music hall ditty that included the line "Here comes the bogey man!" What we call "par" today was once known as "bogey" and born as "ground score". Luckily, the three terms agree---par is the predicted score of a scratch golfer on a specified course under normal weather conditions.

From this common pool of clarity, however, spouts a complex problem. Everyone acknowledges the virtue of a common standard, yet nobody questions the psychological consequences that issue from the application of this standard to players who are anywhere from hailing distance to light years away from scratch. The disconnect between wishful thinking and actual sports performance among amateurs creates a dissonance that can easily collapse into delusion, erratic behavior, and the ever-hovering lover's depression.

No amateur marathon runner would think to base his splits on Olympic class times, yet the average golfer believes he has a sacred duty to match the numbers printed on the scorecard. He strives for a 3 on a par-3, a 4 on a par-4 and a 5 on a par-5, even though he feels these goals are grossly unfair and far beyond his striving. He knows that these numbers are for a "perfect golfer", but he still harbors the irrational fear that shooting over par will somehow exclude his unique thread from the golden fabric of this noble and ancient sport.

In reality the par printed on the card is intended as the projected result for a minute class of golfers---*the less than 1% who are club pros*---yet more than 99% of golfers *take it as a moral imperative.* They believe, independent of their skill or experience, that they *should* shoot par. This collective misunderstanding provokes a rash of self-deprecation and impulsive cheating that erodes self-confidence and fuels a crippling frustration with the game. Golf for the wishful thinker is constant torture. *This is why there are so many joke books on golf and why the term "par" in my golf strategy always means your personal par, not the number on the card.*

The Official Handicap System. The USGA and the Royal & Ancient Golf Club of St. Andrews are impeccably professional organizations dedicated to defending the traditions of golf against inappropriate incursions by modern culture and technology. They are the recognized authorities for any requisite modifications and they attempt to make every amateur competition as fair as possible, including special computer algorithms that can detect scores straying overmuch from standard statistical deviations. They regulate launch speeds of drivers and the depth of wedge grooves with anal intensity. Without question, these two august institutions are fastidiously dedicated to sportsmanship so it's doubly confounding to see official USGA handicaps normally used *as stimulants and authorizations of cheating in American amateur tournaments.*

The philosophy of golf, the spirit that informs every page of the rulebook and every shot at hand, can be succinctly expressed in nine words---*play it as it lies and count every stroke.*

The majority of amateur golfers debase the spirit of the game by cheating in the establishment, maintenance, and application of their official USGA handicaps. You know this small and bitter truth from personal experience. When you enter a tournament away from home you automatically assume your adversaries have manipulated their handicaps to dramatically improve their winning chances. The more important the tournament, the more dishonor and cheating you assume. The situation is perhaps better disguised, but no less grating at your own club. In a term, when it comes to USGA handicaps everybody *else* is a sandbagger.

A handicap golfer is like the guy from Chicago who comes to San Francisco claiming everybody from the Windy City is a liar. Can you believe him? Can you believe Scott Reynolds is a 14? To have a chance with unrepentant cheaters like Scott you're obliged to tweak your own handicap---and you can do it by the book. The USGA calculates your handicap on the best ten of the last twenty rounds submitted, so if you're thinking about the tempting BBQ prizes at the big tournament in Redding you'll obviously leave your good rounds on the table and submit twenty stingers.

This is normal defensive behavior, your opponents are certainly doing far worse. The interesting action actually came before you ever decided which rounds to submit, when the USGA forced you *to stop counting strokes.* All official handicaps come with a safety clause. If your handicap is less than a certain number you're prohibited from marking down more than bogey, double bogey or triple bogey on any hole, no matter how many shots you leave in the trees, sunning in the sand or spinning around the cup. If you're playing poorly, you're commanded by the official ruling body to *violate the basic principle of the game.*

In what other sport can you find such stupendous irony? Your official USGA handicap, based on rounds you select, composed of scores artificially lowered by fiat, is more a lie used to compete with other lies than any reasonable prediction of future results. With the impressive progress in teaching methods and equipment technology official handicaps haven't come down in the past fifty years. The reason for this is that the modern golfer, like his fellow citizens in a big lie society, *is only capable of little lies himself---he limits his lies to acceptable transgressions of his moral code and this limit becomes his official USGA handicap*

The other cheating class. The USGA handicap system also affords another interesting way to cheat. While the majority of amateurs will jack their handicap up so they have a better chance to win a tournament there's also a clever minority that cheats the other way. They submit or fake only *exceptional* scores, which gives them an attractive low handicap. Given that 85% of golfers can't shoot their artificially elevated handicaps in tournaments, this reverse cheating makes sense only when you understand it as a calculated stroke in one of the lesser games. The player who cheats *low* has no intention of actually competing in a golf tournament. He's using that number to *get a contact, get a contract, get a date.*

The Burgess Society. For the knight freedom is a reality won against worthy opponents, harsh circumstances and his own mistakes. As Nietzsche noted, pleasure comes from the feeling that power is growing, and power grows best by overcoming itself. Mistakes are the most fortunate form of truth, the best evidence of personal freedom. Every lie and delusion is a broker of slavery, and the man who comes to prefer the lie by denying the existence or value of his mistakes lives a living death. Slavery becomes the way of least resistance, and propaganda becomes the truth. Fortunately, in golf we have historical antidotes for poisons leaking in from the lesser games. These remedies typically contain a stiff shot of self-reliance. For all their competent administration, the handicap systems of the USGA and R&A make every card-carrying member a collaborator in a big lie.

Like shackled slaves in Plato's cave he sees amateur tournaments come and go like dark shadows on the wall. He comes to depend on the routine announcement of winners that aren't real winners and losers that aren't real losers. Everyone knows it's a sham and eventually the amateur comes to love this Orwellian procession of fakes---manipulated computer-driven handicaps mimic the manipulations of computer-driven New Medieval institutions. Luckily, vigorous response to this falsification of competition can be found in some back issues of golf history. To replace the official handicap systems of the USGA and the R & A, The Burgess Society restores a tournament model invented by an Edinburgh group of the same name in 1862 - 28 years *before* Rotherham invented par.

We divide the Society membership into six categories based on Personal Ground Number and everyone plays straight up inside his category. This PGN is the mathematical average each member keeps of his last 10 rounds, faithfully counting *every stroke and every round.* The member's PGN is his private property---unpublished and inaccessible to the Society, his fellow competitors, or the press without his permission. Our only two requirements for Burgess tournament play are that a member claim a category *on his word of honor* and play by the rules of golf.

Personal honor and fidelity to the spirit of golf gives every amateur member of The Burgess Society the trust and camaraderie that professionals enjoy on tour. When you play worthy opponents every win or loss is authentic. When you play by the rules you can overcome harsh circumstance and monumental mistakes. *Given the proper conditions we are all free and honorable men.*

The Concept Of Personal Par For Amateurs. To strategize a new round start with your Personal Ground Number. First subtract the scorecard par from your PGN. The remainder is your Personal Strategy Number. For example, if your PGN is 90 and par for Glendover Woods is 71 your PSN is 19. You then distribute the 19 strokes *as you like* on the eighteen holes to find your personal par for each hole. Say there's a long par 4 that gives you trouble. You can make it a personal par of 7 and have 16 stokes left to distribute on the remaining seventeen holes.

Think of scorecard hole ranking as a double dose of the "perfect golfer's" par. The only reason these numbers are on the card is so handicap players can know where to give and take their concocted strokes. Find the time to write your own hole ranking over these numbers. Maybe #2 has a long carry off the tee, or a dogleg into the wind, or a triple level green that habitually gives you trouble. Research your past rounds on the same course under similar weather conditions and note the holes where you usually score well and those where you typically explode. With this empirical data you'll know how to scientifically distribute your PSN and your personal pars for today's round.

When strategizing with your PSN trust your records and let your imagination fly. Try hitting two eight-irons to a par-3, three five-irons to a par-4, or two hybrids, a six-iron and a sand wedge to a par-5. When you know what you're doing you always have a better chance of pulling it off. Remember---*par always means your personal par and personal birdie means the wide world applauds your being-here.*

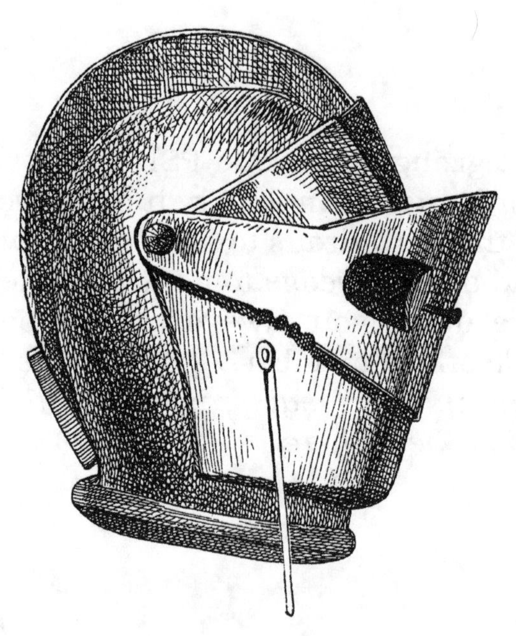

The Concept Of Personal Par For Touring Pros. Calculate your PGN, PSN and personal pars realistically. If you're in the top third of the money list your PGN is around 70. This means you need to designate two holes---usually, but not necessarily par-5s---where scorecard birdie is your personal par. Thus, in applying the third part of the Second Rule, if you are playing poorly and go 5-over your *personal par,* which is three over scorecard par, you must immediately start playing every hole for birdie. If you're having a poor season and your PGN is over 72 you need to designate a hole or two where scorecard bogey is your personal par. It's essential for the touring pro in danger of losing his playing card to bite this bullet of false pride.

Wishful thinking, frozen memories of better times or ill-suppressed anger won't get you back to the top of the leaderboard. You need a conscientious plan. If you make scorecard par on your designated hole it's a personal birdie and you're playing the next hole for birdie. As your PGN improves these bogey-pars evaporate, and you can rediscover the pleasure of designating birdies as personal pars. *The Monday qualifier exception.* Independent of your current PGN and the results of the year to date, if you are playing a large number of pros for one or two spots in a tournament the odds have already made you 5 over par so *your only logical strategy is to play every hole for birdie.*

The Center Line. In chess there are two types of planning---positional and combinational. To win a chess game you first take control of the four squares in the center of the board and then organize an attack on your opponent's king. Position necessarily precedes combination. In Formula 1 racing you steer a knife-edge line through the curves, and displacement from that center line through inattention, collision, or mechanical failure ends your race. In billiards you try to position the cue ball in the middle of the table to maximize your options for the next shot. In football you must dominate the ten yards surrounding the line of scrimmage in order to run or pass with any efficiency. Control of a Center Line or Central Space is a strategic necessity in most games and sports. In golf, the Center Line is drawn on the scorecard by the architect. It's the most efficient path your ball can travel from tee to green. Once you position your ball on the Center Line with a drive or second you can plan combinational attacks on the green with *lethal* serenity.

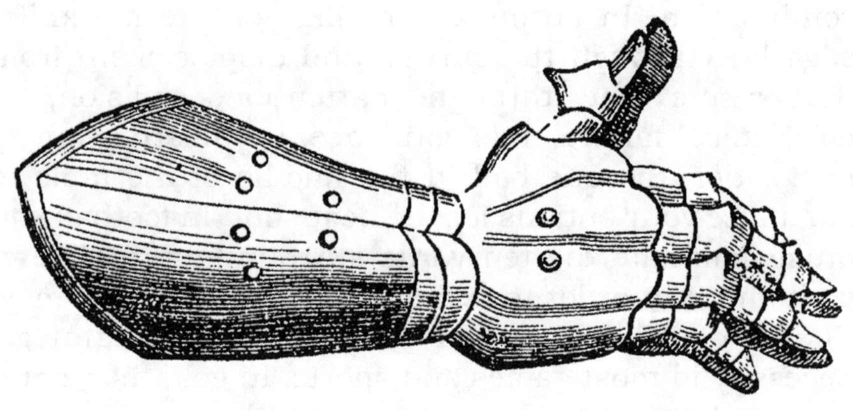

When To Move The Line. The Center Line can be redrawn for tactical reasons. If you're coming off double bogey *move the end of the Center Line off the green to the safest greenside fringe* so you have an easy chip and par putt. If you're coming off birdie, hit your drive to a point on the Center Line beyond the angle of the dogleg and *move the end of the Center Line to the cup.* When you're hot it's *your* job to turn up the heat.

Locura
Locura.
Desconaerto
Auctor.
Querer.
Poco sesa
Auentura
El Brado del Plaser mundano.

Playing for birdie. The house grinds you down. Ask any gambler or bureaucrat. If you stay in your seat too long you lose. That's why you have to take full advantage of positive trends, those elusive waves of clarity when things are going well. You increase the size of your bet, you take the 3-point jumper from downtown, you gun the long downhill birdie putt. Because golf is a game where bad things happen often, optimal golf strategy minimizes the effects of bad play and bad bounces until you can psychologically recover.

The Second Rule combines the best defense with the best offense. The physical rush, the mental elation that wins golf tournaments comes from *stringing some birdies together.* Remember, attempting birdie after a bogey or worse is a fool's play, a grandstand gesture announcing, "I want to quit this damned game and I might as well start now!"

It's equally foolish to play timidly or conservatively after making birdie. Trying to protect your birdie and bring it back safely to the clubhouse in a pretty nest of limegreen moss and small twigs is a serious strategic blunder. It's the error journeyman pros make on a daily basis. For them every birdie has a certain cash value, it guarantees a certain chunk of a check. A champion like Tiger Woods or Phil Mickelson knows the best use of a birdie---or eagle---is to get the warrior blood flowing. He sees things better now, he's looser now, he's thinking sharper now. He instinctively knows this is the moment for the kill. Put in vernacular---*to win you have to grow bigger testicles as you approach the final holes.*

This masculine truth is well illustrated at the World Series Of Poker as the final table starts to shake out a winner. The tight technicians who get to the final felt by exploiting the desperation of weak players can't change gears, can't adapt to the looser requirements and craziness of a short table. They're taken out by gunslingers with the gonads to play any two cards for $10 Million. If he can smell the win the knight closes the deal, even if he has to do things he's never done before. He invents, he improvises, he changes gears, he rides the rush. Making par is great, but a realist knows he's not the only one who gets hot. Winning a golf tournament usually means *making more birdies on your rush than your fellow competitors do on theirs.*

So how do you practice making birdie? By making the birdie putt a demonstration of your resolve. Despite the diligence of Dave Pelz and Allan Strand, the strategic importance of putting is generally minimized by the vast majority of teaching pros. Some impetus for this oversight, of course, comes from the students themselves. Like Japanese workers on lunchtime rooftops, golf practice in the minds of most American golfers has come to mean banging out balls on the driving range. This attitude is encouraged and abetted by teaching pros that depend on range lessons for a large slice of their livelihood.

It's all about proper diagnosis. The pro's job, as he sees it, is *to keep you in the game.* Every student they see is ready to quit. Like a cognitive therapist whose goal is to get his client back to work within the timeframe set by the insurance company, the teaching pro has specific and limited goals. Within a forty-five minute window he has to diagnose his client's most damaging swing flaw, walk him through a plausible correction and convince him that recovery is just a day away. Is Saturday at 10 or Sunday at 3 better for you?

PGA and LPGA pros are well-trained to teach swing mechanics. They can diffuse the desperation of a depressed golfer by reviewing the fundamentals of the golf swing step by step. Students are encouraged to conclude that swing speed and launch angle are the gates to paradise because nothing beyond mechanics is offered. If a student were to ask, “I’m tired of losing to my pals at work, can you teach me how to win?” he’d typically be answered with a shrug and a smile. Here’s the catch. By confining lessons to the range, teaching pros, in the name of their own economic convenience, *doom their clients to losing.* Hitting balls on the range without purpose *has the least strategic value in golf.* If you want to win golf tournaments you have to immediately become a master of the short stick.

In the 90s I had the good fortune to work with Pat Fitzsimons. We created The Art Of Scoring Golf School and conducted a golf talk show on local radio. We gave short game clinics in Oregon and one hot summer session at The Resort At The Mountain was especially memorable. The students were alert during the lectures and quickly understood their short game options during the on-course session. We had a social putting tournament to finish with a flourish, and only over a glass of closing champagne did the oddness hit.

A well-dressed couple from Miami approached and said *sotto voce*, "Your golf school was interesting and very informative. We had lots of fun. We both feel much more confident with our wedge and putter now, but we just have to say something. Why didn't we get to go to the range? We attend five or six of the best golf schools in the country every year and this is the first time we were kept from the range. Please don't contact us again."

An immediate survey, even more *sotto voce*, confirmed this opinion from other attendees. After the shock and the bubbly wore off Pat and I realized our mistake---in presenting a new way to learn golf we'd overlooked the possibility that students would prefer to stay buried in the old. We wanted to show them a new way to lower their score and they walked through it mindlessly waiting to hit range balls. The fact that it was billed as a short game clinic and the resort didn't have a driving range was immaterial. We'd overestimated our audience. Why?

You know why. Because most people prefer not to think, and once they believe they know something they don't ever want to think about it again. Because most people like to follow. Like to ride. Like to hide in the crowd. The modern golf driving range is a working metaphor for the grazing range. Where the sheep feed. Where competitive golf dreams go to die. I'd been too soft. I'm a teacher, not an entertainer. And I didn't do what needed to be done. I didn't shake them up, didn't wake them up. Our professional demeanor allowed them to continue in their semi-conscious routines. As you'll see soon, what happened at Welches has had a strong influence on the development of my system.

Praising, coddling and selling the next lesson are insults to your intelligence. If you want to play *at* golf, if you want to evade what I'm saying in this book by reading something else I strongly suggest you avoid the great 1959 predecessor of this work, *Play A Round Of Golf With Tommy Armour.* Tommy was the highest paid teaching pro of his era and the tongue-lashing he gives Bill, a rich member of Boca Raton ranting to quit the game, deserves a fifty-year run on Broadway. Tommy created a radical new teaching method for his or any other time---he challenged his clients to use their brains. He knew how many major tournaments on the PGA Tour, how many $100 nassaus at the club were lost from sheer stupidity.

Even with Tommy doing the thinking for him, Bill, the millionaire businessman, reverts to his lazy mental habits at every opportunity. He stops thinking after good shots. He stops thinking after bad ones. He crows and flatters when things are going well, scowls and curses when things are not, constantly talking about his latest business coup. Tommy's so frustrated with Bill's inability to overcome his self-destructive emotions and play smart golf that he breaks the lesson off at the turn and hits the bar to ask a few shots of unblended why he can't keep a fool's brain alive for more than nine holes.

The Graduate School of Golf. GSG functions like an academic graduate school for professional and amateur golfers. We assume entering students have learned sound swing mechanics, course management skills, and sports psychology in their previous golf education. We complete their study of golf by concentrating on tournament performance. All of our advanced courses in golf strategy and strategic practice are designed to give students a decisive advantage in competition. Every word, every lesson, every round is focused on victory, thus the only two prerequisites for admission are a keen desire to win and a good working knowledge of the rules of golf.

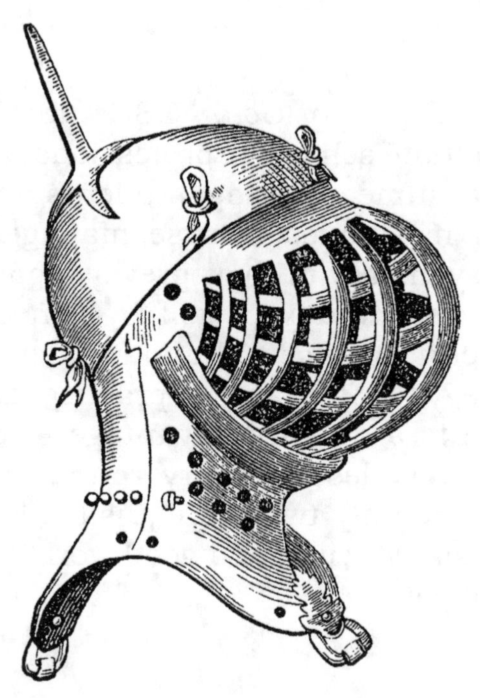

The Graduate School Of Golf Strategic Practice Program

1. The two-foot putt
2. The six-foot putt
3. Long putts
4. Greenside artistry
5. The First Point
6. The Second Point
7. Medium and long approaches
8. The Third Point

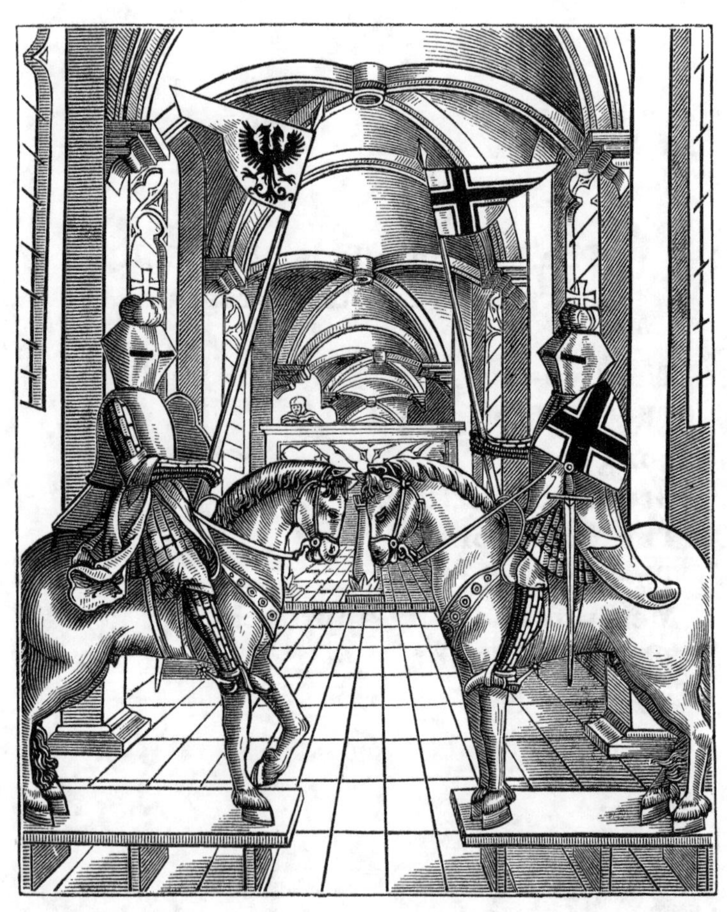

The GSG practice program is designed to support the Johns Golf Strategy. Your first test is to make 36 two-foot birdie putts in a row. This can be done anywhere. On the practice green, at the office, at home. When I started my first golf school in the early 80s I rambled the LA freeways with a Roger Dunn Astroturf putting green in the trunk of my 67 Chrysler 300. Every lesson began with two-footers and today, after 25 years of teaching golf, every session still begins with the two-footers. When you can sink 36 in a row as smoothly as pouring a glass of beer, move your target number up to 54. Then 72. The anxiety of having to start over from 1 after missing simulates the hyperbolic nature of short putts in tournament play. When the pressure is intense, the ordinary becomes extraordinary so a key objective of the GSG practice program *is to make the pressure a pleasure.*

Every golfer can become automatic with a two-foot putt. Just step up, keep your head down and knock them in. Use any putter you want. Use your high school blade. Use a Scotty Cameron. Use the rusty rake you found in a Napa wine barrel. Use one of those new titanium spaceships. Whatever empirically works. I've been using Allan Strand's Dandy putter since it was introduced and find it puts the best roll on the ball. Especially on fast greens. Once you can make 72 straight two-footers with your favorite putter you're done. Making short putts is now a part of your golfing identity, *and playing strategically to your personal pars will give you several two-foot birdie putts a round.*

A six-foot putt is only three times longer than the two-footer, but a hundred times harder to make. On the meticulously manicured greens of the PGA Tour professionals make about 50% of their six-footers. Amateurs playing on municipal greens with uneven maintenance and the usual lumpy donut around the hole can normally expect to make around 30%. The GSG test requires the student to sink 20 of 36 six-footers. I want you to parlay the confidence you earned with two-footers into comfort with the longer putt. Attention!---the six-foot putt is *strategically the single most important stroke in golf.* If a touring pro makes 100% of his six-footers over four days he wins a major. If you make 60% of your six-footers in the Zonal you'll probably qualify for the Burgess National Championships.

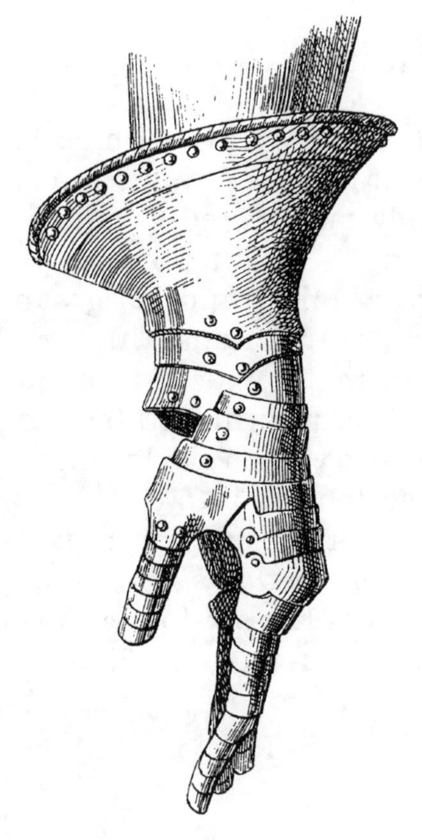

The long putts are strictly a matter of pace. Your goal is to get the ball into your two-foot automatic zone. If the distance is formidable and the undulations insidious, your secondary target becomes the six-foot zone. If you're having persistent trouble with pace you might consider adding a heavier putter to your bag. The same putter that works well at two and six feet may not have the right feel at forty or seventy. Until the 30s pros had a putter in their bag for every distance and condition---lofted putters for gnarly greens, light putters for the fast short putts and heavy putters for the slow long putts. Some years ago The Burgess Society repealed the fourteen club rule, so our members carry as many putters as they like.

Practice your greenside artistry with the same objectives as the long putts. Chipping, pitching, flops, and sand explosions should settle in your automatic two-foot putting zone. If the shot has a high degree of difficulty your secondary target should again be the six-foot zone. GSG students are asked to create their own tests here because they know best which situations and conditions give them the most trouble. Try devising a customized skills test for your greenside art in the comfort of your home course---you'll be surprised to learn which ones are actually causing you the most pain.

The entire area surrounding the green is your canvas. Your wedges are your brushes. Your recovery is your signature. *You'll know your greenside recovery shots are fine art when your signature is the same on every hole.*

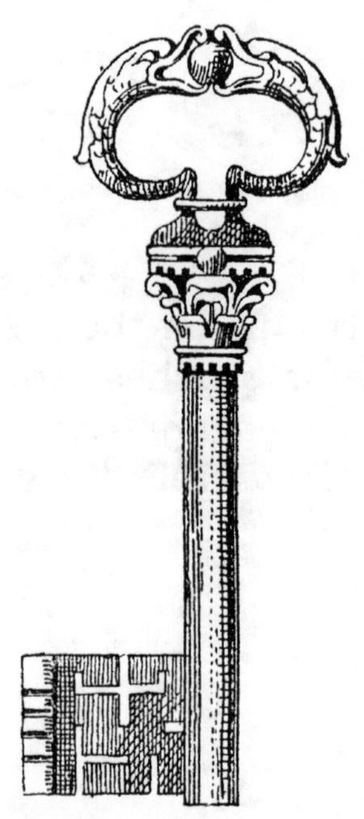

The First Point. Somewhere twenty to thirty yards from the green is a perfect spot for your wedge. This is your First Point. It can be a lob, sand, or pitching wedge. Choose the club that statistically works the best for you. Hit fifty balls to the green from this zone with a hard swing and identify your optimal distance. I want you so comfortable at your First Point that you don't see or even sense the bunkers and lakes protecting the green. I want you automatic, like a two-footer. The GSG test is 7 out of 10 balls within twenty feet. Once you pass, the First Point is officially yours. It's your balmy tropical island in a snarling green sea of menace, your intermediary target for any shot up the fairway or rough.

By identifying and claiming your First Point you've eliminated 95% of the disasters that come from fear, indecision and half-swings around the green. After a smooth fruit cocktail and a midnight swim with your lover you can approach the green without anxiety. *When you're feeling great it's easy to knock it stiff from your First Point.*

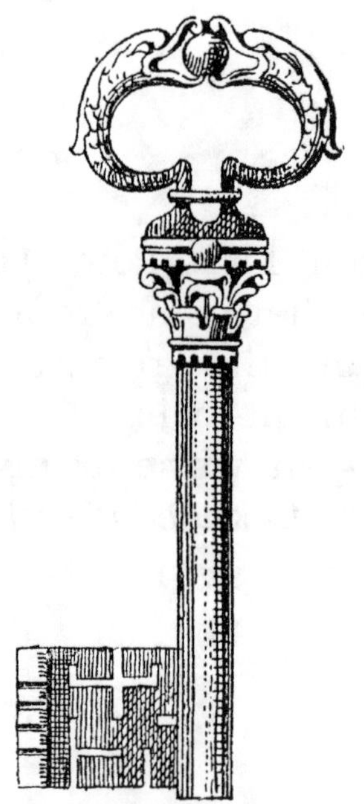
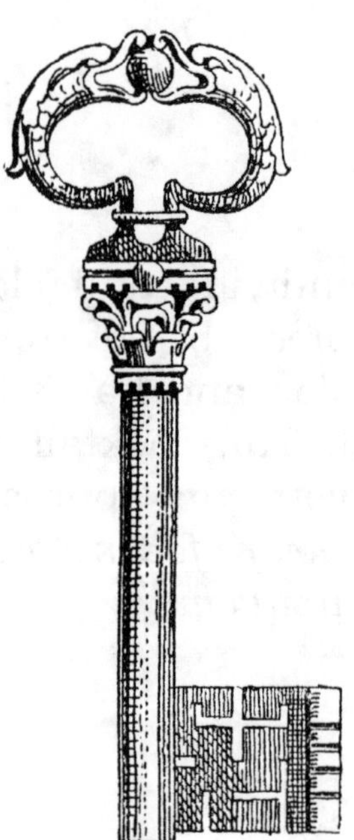

Your Second Point is from ninety to a hundred yards out. Again, hit fifty balls with a hard swing to the green from this zone with any club you like and find the distance that works best for you. The GSG test is 4 of 10 balls within twenty feet. Once you pass, the Second Point is also yours. You now own a second piece of paradise amidst the howling squalls of uncertainty. A second private island becomes a target option for any shot up the fairway or rough. Standing on the fairway at Pebble Beach Graeme McDowell knew par would win so he hit a seven-iron to his Second Point and cruised to vistory at the 2010 US Open with a wedge and two putts.

Seen through the lens of individual freedom, the tees, fairways, and greens of golf all change their appearance to fit the progression of the seasons but your First and Second Points are always perfect, always waiting to serve. This personal geometry is the reality you superimpose on Nature. Your points are the intersections of your creative will with the wide world. As Heidegger concludes, the power of this art is what makes your being-here *here.*

Wind & Lie. After mastering the use of your First and Second Points I work on medium and long approaches. You study the wind. You learn to recognize swirls and gusts. You learn how headwinds, sidewinds, and tailwinds affect spin in the air and roll after shots hit the ground. You study the terrain. You become a geographer, a geologist, a gardener. You learn how sidehill lies, downhill lies, and uphill lies affect spin and roll. You learn to escape terrible lies, so a bad break becomes your lever to the win. To sharpen their shot-shaping and course management skills students are referred to two fine books---1981's *Jack Nicklaus' Playing Lessons* and 1993's *Tom Watson's Strategic Golf.* Once again, GSG students compose their own skill tests, practicing difficult approaches from the rough or trees. *When you practice the impossible you perfect the possible.*

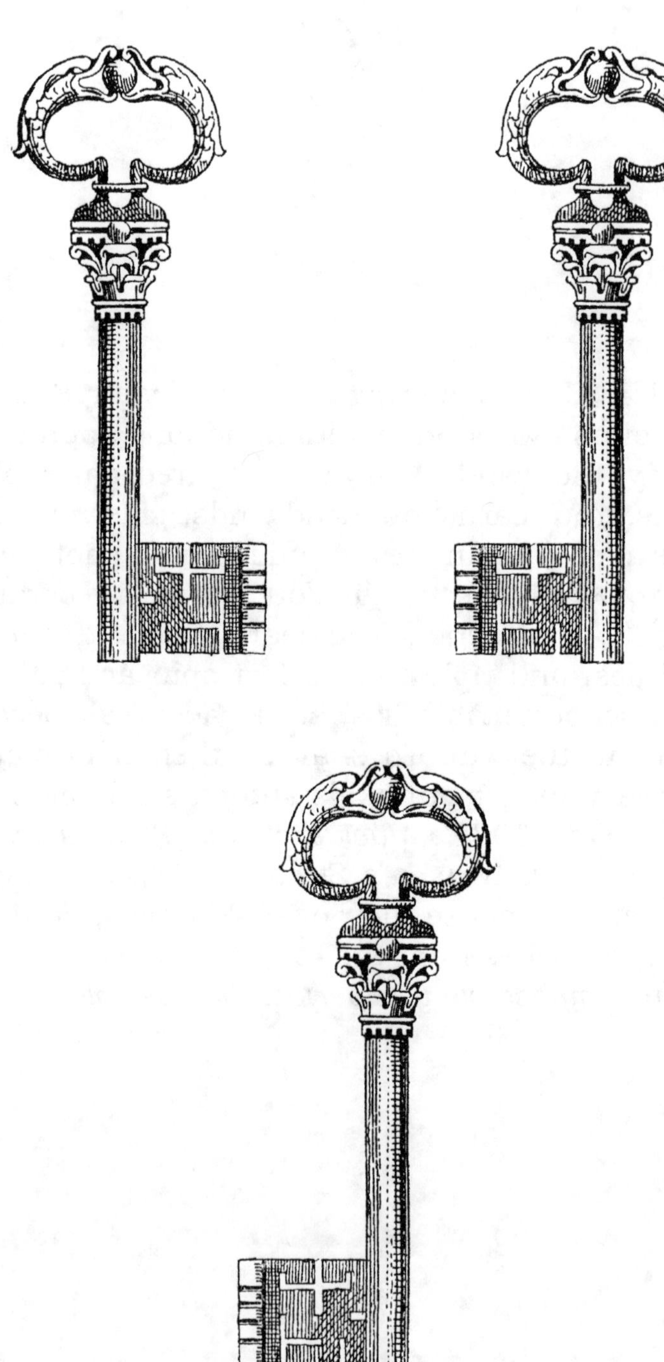

The GSG Strategic Practice Program finishes at the tee box, where students learn that the only good reason to be on the driving range is to be fine-tuning your Third Point. Throughout his great career Sam Snead used a 3-wood or a driver tweaked to fifteen degrees off the tee to transform his natural power into distance control. Your Third Point is where you can place 7 of 10 tee shots in the fairway and pass the test. For most players this Third Point is normally 200 to 250 yards out, but for the longer hitters it can stretch to 280 and morc.

You'll need to monitor your Third Point carefully because---unlike your First and Second Points---it constantly moves. Beginners and juniors may find their Third Point extending out ten yards a week as they progress. They might start hitting 7 of 10 in the fairway at 150 yards and eventually stabilize a month later at 250. It can also go the other way. If you're a touring pro and you're not hitting your Third Point at 290, shorten your swing, change your driver or open your stance to get the required accuracy.

Today's high-tech drivers are exotic Ferraris offering tantalizing power and beauty, but if it were a matter of *life-or-death* and you had to take your mother to the emergency room in a snowstorm, you'd want to feel absolutely sure the Ferrari could get her there. Otherwise you'd take the Suburu. Remember Sam Snead. On the tee box the knight is the embodiment of reason and he selects his weapon accordingly.

After the six-foot putt, the drive is the most strategic shot in golf. The new USGA wedge groove regulations mean drive and slash as a tactic will be reserved for Monday qualifiers because you won't be able to stick it from the rough. The premium will be on driving accuracy, which logically increases the strategic value of your Third Point. While others are mindlessly hacking through buckets of balls on the range, you'll be fine-tuning your competitive advantage. Once you pass the driving test the GSG strategic practice program is over. Yes, it's difficult. By design. I want you so confident over the ball that making the shots dictated by strategy in tournament play is *easy, second nature.* At The Graduate School Of Golf every concept, every word, every lesson is focused on victory---*and you don't graduate until you win.*

The knight is a future mounted on a past, his sword the true intelligence.

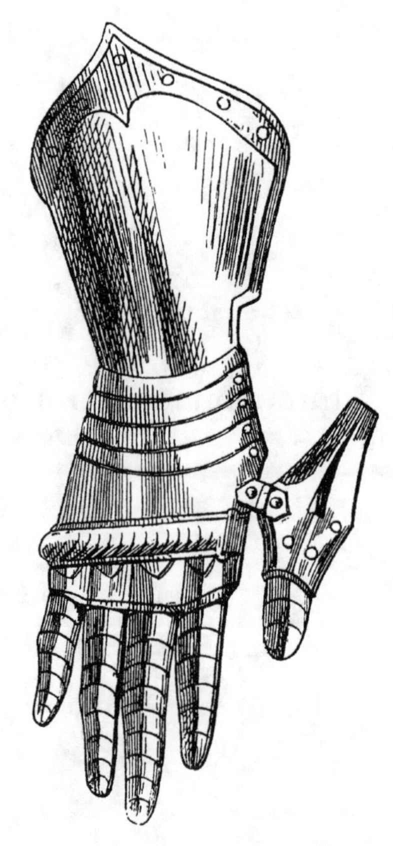

The Stranger. As your golf knowledge improves the stranger called happiness will become a more welcome guest at your table. A good way to celebrate the arrival of this golfing pleasure is to challenge a good friend to a match. Feel the wind, the grass, the click of the clubface as it meets the ball. What happened to those wild swings of unpredictable passion? What happened to the churning stomach and the sweaty brow? What happened to the temptation to shave a stroke?

After the round celebrate with your friend at the bar, and then challenge a player you despise. The one who coughs on your backswing, the one who takes every putt inside the leather. Yes, *that* one. Feel your new severity and serenity. Feel your new golf freedom transcend his semi-consciousness. His ignorance. His negligence. His crude and transparent attempts at gamesmanship. Now you enter true warrior mentality and confront every future threat, every mysterious opponent with the killer instinct. This is the New Medieval. Who knows what Red Dragon awaits? What bloodthirsty Black Knight? What mythical Green Knight hungry for your head?

The Psychic Origins Of Golf. Much has been speculated about the historical origins of golf. Some claim it was born in China, some in Rome, some think it bloomed like yellow tulips beside the icy canals of Holland. The actual birthplace of golf is moot, because history strongly suggests that the spirit of the game has been developed by the personality of the Scots. Wherever golf is played in the world there's always a faint echo of bagpipes in the air. Thrifty by necessity, romantic by nature, the Scots have earned the right over the last seven hundred years to be considered caretakers of the game.

Under this kilt, however, is a central psychic event that predates the Scots and evokes the Greek roots of Western Civilization. A dark secret hiding so well in plain sight that its effect on the Western mind is missed by the keenest observers---*playing golf is about going into the earth and coming out again.*

Western culture has witnessed the overthrow of the chthonic gods---the deities of the earth and the nether regions---in favor of sun and sky gods. In the mysteries at Eleusis Dionysus carried a fennel club and went down into the earth to suffer dismemberment and ultimate revival so Nature could renew itself. So Spring could *be*. Could the psychic origins of the modern golf experience be grounded in this ancient Greek rite? Man is the ball, man must go underground. Consider this---why is every golfer so anxious to get his ball out of the cup? What does he fear? Does he shrink from the memory of falling through to the land of infinite shadow? Why the dread? Why the trembling grip on the small white sphere?

Considered mythically, a round of golf is eighteen trips to hell and back. It's the mysterious, primordial Western thrill---a rite of initiation, a forgotten language of animal dismemberment speaking directly to the heart. It's the perennial allure, the siren song of personal annihilation underground. It's a flash of every man's future. It's an old ritual acted out in the complex and troubled mind of modern man, and it confirms the locker room insight that a golfer's deepest relief after finishing a round *is finding his arms and legs intact.*

Bad holes and bad rounds are essential components of the game so it's important for every competitor to keep cool under psychological duress. Any single hole played thoughtlessly today *damages all the future holes you play for the rest of your life.* Everyone has a tendency to give up when disaster strikes, to pretend it's not really happening, to block it out. Always be thinking. Always be learning. The knight learns something from every mistake. He learns best from his biggest mistakes. If bad play gets him five over par it becomes a golden door, an invitation to open up. He either recovers from the disasters of the day or polishes his aggressive play for the next time it's required.

Two Anomolies. Throughout this book I've presumed a strong will to win. There are also, however, certain situations where you need to reverse basic strategy---when you're playing to lose and when you're not playing to score. To illustrate, in the mid 80s I had a prominent Japanese-American client in LA who was hosting an important superior from Tokyo. My client was an active player at Bel Air Country Club, proud of his USGA handicap of "15". My mission was to teach him *how to lose* to his superior without appearing to do so. The fact that the big boss had a handicap of "45" complicated the case considerably. The solution was obtained by reversing basic strategy. My client hit his expensive new driver wildly on every tee. He missed every six-footer on the low side. After every bad hole he played angrily and aggressively. His boss never suspected the truth and invited my client out to one of LA's best nightclubs to celebrate the upset in the company of *his* boss.

In the early 90s I was the club pro at Il Picciolo Golf Club in Sicily. This exclusive club, perched on the lava shoulders of Mt. Etna, was administered by a leading family of the region. A tight circle of friends organized the typical menu of club tournaments. Tuesday might be a men's medal, Wednesday a mixed foursomes, Saturday a scramble. As the club pro my job was to help every member perform well in these events, which, due to local custom, were conducted *as if scoring was the most random face of golf.* One vivacious Carla, who summered in Paris and Edinburgh, had a personal vendetta against putting. Everyone who played in her foursome was forbidden to count strokes after the ball kissed the green. As you can easily imagine, there was a considerable amount of genteel jousting to join her foursome before it was announced.

After any tournament was completed there were thirty minutes of back room suspense while the tournament directors discussed *which type of tournament had actually been played.* It was not unusual to see medal play turn like quicksilver into match and re-emerge triumphant as Scotch foursomes, with the club members unanimously applauding the delicacy of the decision. The strong personalities in the inner circle always won, nobody really lost, and the wine and food were superb. Under these elegant local variations and special circumstances I discarded the notion of scoring altogether and taught the pure aesthetics of the golf shot---how to dress, how to make a graceful turn, how to test the wind with five blades of grass.

At the time I thought it was merely picaresque that no Italian had served as teaching professional at Il Picciolo. There'd been an Englishman, an Irishman, and now an American. Why no Italians? The members of this elegant club were all powerful Sicilians in the Sicilian manner, but they were ultimately hamstrung by Italian bureaucracy. They'd paid a handsome sum for their membership and weren't allowed to play on their own golf course until they'd passed a difficult and comprehensive national skills test *administered by the club pro.*

Well, nobody in his right mind would consider flunking one of these esteemed gentlemen, and none of them was close to passing the test legitimately. Worse, Sicily is an island where gossip has religious power, and any slack I gave one member would immediately be reported to another with baroque embellishments. I was on a rock, between a hard place and no-place. Happily, a working solution presented itself through a simple reinterpretation of the text. The national test was supposed to be taken in a single day so I decided to string it out over three months or more.

I'd take a member onto the course in a golf cart and casually introduce him to putting, the greenside arts, bunker play, fairway woods and the other elements of the test. When a member happened to pass one part of it, "Bravo Guido!" and eventually every member of Il Picciolo was happily playing on the course. *The real comedy is consciousness, the sources of our best ideas are often the most challenging events of our lives. The practice plan I improvised in Sicily is the one you're reading right now.*

The Third Rule is play the last hole for par unless you need birdie to win. If you're leading by one or more, playing for par forces your competitors into risk because you take bogey out of play. If you're tied or behind by one or more play for birdie. A win is always a thousand times more valuable than a place, never assume your competitors will fail to execute *their* strategies. Playing for birdie when you're behind is obvious. It's tougher to gear down for par on #18 when you're coming *off* birdie. The most notorious example of eighteenth hole mind-lock was submitted by French journeyman Jean Van de Velde on the last hole of the 1999 British Open at Carnoustie.

After 71 holes of scintillating play Van De Velde came to #18 knowing he only needed double-bogie to win. A four-iron and two wedges would've done the job nicely. As it transpired Van de Velde was so transfixed by his emotions coming off birdie, and the memory of making two previous birdies on the hole he couldn't gear down. He hit driver to the right rough, then hit the grandstands, Barry's Burn, a bunker and eventually made a difficult six-footer for triple-bogie. He went on to lose the playoff and become the most extravagant symbol of thoughtlessness in the long history of golf. *To this day Van de Velde doesn't remember what happened at Carnoustie. If you're not using your mind when you compete there's nothing to remember later.*

Hunter, warrior, knight. Let's dig a little deeper. Perhaps the core experience of golf predates the Greeks. Hundreds of thousands of years earlier than the inventions of agriculture, government and literature we were nomadic hunters and the men went out to kill game. If the hunt was unsuccessful it could prove fatal to himself, his family, and his clan. At the very least a series of bad hunts meant the tribe would have to move on to unproven hunting grounds. If he was after deer, caribou or the massive aurochs he could still bring home a wild pig or rabbit to polite applause. To return empty handed was total humiliation, a complete loss of being-here.

If you have friends on the PGA or LPGA Tours you know this hunter mentality is still very much alive in professional golf, particularly a notch off the top. The international stars of golf are well-represented by business managers who procure a safety net of lucrative endorsement deals and appearance fees. If you're a golf celebrity with some big pelts under your saddle you can command amazing numbers for corporate outings and promotional engagements. The tyro or journeyman on tour, however, has only one way to survive---eat what he kills.

If he misses the cut in Orlando his family back in Salt Lake City suffers exponentially. If he misses several cuts in a row, he'll be getting calls and text messages from his wife. The Honda dealer needs a new car manager. Glendover Woods has an opening for an assistant pro. It takes a lot of courage to stay with the hunt until the kill. The pro's playing *life-or-death* out there, and he doesn't have a bench to ride.

Professional football, basketball, baseball, and hockey players have multi-million dollar guaranteed contracts. If they break an arm or leg, they're still well paid to frown on the sidelines. The second-tier touring pro has to directly challenge the void every time he plays. If he's injured, he's lost. If he allows the pressure to swamp him, he's lost. If his wife doesn't return a call, he's lost. If his kids forget his name he still has to tee it up against a hundred and fifty of the best hunters in the world *every week*. Like our prehistoric ancestors, unless he has a hunting strategy that works under "kill or move on" pressure he'll collapse into superstition. The hot driver. The hot conditioning program. The touted swing guru. The new magnetic bracelet. The new talisman. He'll try anything, because the innermost pride of a professional golfer *is the hunter's will to provide for his family.*

Five Aphorisms On Strategy

1. To think life is only strategy is a big mistake. To think life is only strategy and mistakes is a bigger mistake. To think life is an indefinite series of strategies and mistakes is a joke close to the truth.

2. The mark of a good strategy is to disappear in our intimate moments. The mark of a great strategy is to disappear in our public ones.

3. Life is a rush of violent stratagems over a plain of strategic calm.

4. Because all strategy is survival we find it easier to survive the future than the past.

5. Those without the foresight to adopt a strategy are quickly adopted by one.

Tournaments & War. The word *tournament* was first used in the 11th Century to describe mock battles French and English knights fought on large tracts of open ground to keep themselves in combat shape. The winner was the last mounted knight and the dehorsed loser was forced to give up his weapons and armor. The theory of every game and sports tournament we play today is rooted in these bloody Medieval melees. The fact that we're even talking about golf strategy and playing golf tournaments means we're not fighting a World War or recovering from nuclear devastation.

The knight is opposed to the computerized slaughter of modern war because it has abolished respect for the enemy. The knight directs his will to defeat the advent and ascendancy of modern warfare because it presents the greatest real threat to his chivalric honor. Under martial or military law the knight's personal code is compromised by presidents and generals, under theocratic law his genius is compromised by priests and police. By choosing tournaments over war, honor over self-interest, *golfers are a strong and abiding force for peace.*

Variations For Match Play. In the 13th Century the joust was introduced to tournaments. Instead of one-against-the-field it was one-against-one, two charging knights attempting to unhorse each other with one blow of the lance. In game theory terms it's zero-sum---if I win you lose, if you win I lose. Head-to-head competition in golf is popular in important amateur tournaments and at traditional clubs so the question logically arises---*how can the Johns Golf Strategy be adapted to match play?*

In match play Watson counsels to play safely if your opponent's in trouble and play aggresively if you're in trouble. The flaw in this common way of thinking is that by paying constant attention to the play of your opponent you take focus away from your own game. In match play you're close to your opponent, you can see and read his face. You're not competing against a large abstract field of fellow competitors---you're competing directly against *him.* You'll find a way to dislike him. You'll search for a way to throw him off his game. You'll come to hate him when he's addressing a shot.

This demonization of the enemy comes directly from the propaganda of war, religion, politics and the other lesser games. In the NBA and NFL it's trash-talking. You assume your enemy is a devil so you can justify any barbaric behavior or idea that assists your fighting frenzy. Research the insane propaganda of the past World Wars. Dialectically, demonization of the enemy leads to torture and sado-masochism. Do you really want these base perspectives influencing your golf game?

In match play *ignore* your opponent. Think of him as just another fellow competitor. Stick to the strategy. Play the J. A hole in match play is worth from 2 to 3 times a stroke in medal play, so if you're 3 down at any time in the match, or 2 down with 7 to play, play for birdie in. If you keep your mind on your game you'll be immune to the unpredictable emotional swings caused by his good or bad shots. If you watch him too closely, he's certain to pull off a miracle somewhere. As the knight you want *all* of your opponent's shots to come off---*so you can top them.*

Variations For Women. Throughout Western history women have also distinguished themselves as hunters, warriors, and knights. The classical Greeks were more intimidated by the wild Amazons than the entire Persian army. Joan of Arc is recognized by the French as their national inspiration, their highest military genius. In the Burgess Society women compete freely in all six categories against men, boys and girls. In the current year we have two distaff National Champions, Victoria Susan and Victoria Linda. In the wide world men and women are legally and morally equal but within the aesthetics of our golf society one characteristic is clearly distinct---when a woman has a win in her jaws she becomes a lioness.

No amount of graduate education can dissuade a man's instinctive sense of sportsmanship from rising up to dissipate an advantage when competing against a woman. We find a woman's cultural advantage when competing against men is abundantly compensated by a strong disadvantage when playing against the sophisticated emotional ploys of boys and girls. No amount of graduate education can escape the subtle extortions encountered when competing against the young. When playing kids keep your emotional distance or *their deep bag of tricks will eventually bring out the sacrificial mother in you.*

Joan of Arc was the greatest knight of the Old Medieval. She believed only in the voice of Will To Power. Dressed as a man she ignored the moribund dogmas of military commanders and church authorities. Dressed in steel she ignored the wagging tongues of polite society. Her will crowned a king and bore a nation. Her military valor revalued the goal of war and transformed a game of ransom into the modern concept of the win. Joan invented war strategy and she knew what she was doing at all times. Captured by the English she was immediately abandoned by the French generals she'd led to unexpected victory at Orleans. At her trial in 1461 she was given the choice of life in an English prison or the stake. She chose the fire. She was 19. She invented Napoleon and what Western Civilization now calls *total victory*.

My best student. In 1998 the Dr. Lawrence Johns Golf Academy, then at Persimmon Country Club, was ranked #1 in the state of Oregon. As a pleasant consequence of this recognition a cub reporter from The Business Journal came out to do a piece. Elaine was fresh out of journalism school at the University of Oregon and had never held a golf club in her life. This was Mozart to my ears. I talked to her about golf game theory, I gave her a crash course in strategic practice at the learning facility, and then we played the course. With native athletic grace and intellectual curiosity she went around in 44. Every word I said she heard, every technique I demonstrated she could copy flawlessly. Afterwards she was modestly disappointed she hadn't shot 36. In her subsequent article for the Journal she spoke eloquently about the smell of the flowers, the oceanic undulations of the fairways, the *sweet simplicity of putting the ball into the hole.*

Variations for Seniors. To win in Burgess competition seniors have to get a good grip on their stories. Sure, you used to drive even with the oak tree on #7, sure you sank that fifteen-footer to win the Texas Amateur. These real events become fish tales over time and need to be erased because they're quickly followed by darker images of snapping three drives in a row OB on #15, yipping nine consecutive two-footers and a nightmarish compendium of lame shots cropping up at the most embarrassing moments. When competing against younger men, women, and kids in your class you're always the underdog, so to win you have no choice but to out-practice, out-cool, and out-strategize them. Never think of your winning story before it happens---*because it takes too long to come back.*

Variations for Juniors. The natural advantage of young golfers is that they are so tremendously infused with immortality that they can play *life-or-death* golf at a fever pitch for every hole of the tournament. Communication with their muscles is so seamless that all they have to do is send a simple impulse to pull off a great shot. That's why learning strategy and practicing strategically is never premature in a golf career. *There's no minimum age for knights.* The LPGA Tour is blessed with a large number of teenagers from around the world who compete weekly at the highest level. The main variation for juniors is reducing the number of required drives in the fairway from 7 to 5 when fine-tuning their Third Point. You should always be stretching your limits. Keep bashing the ball---*without the bashing sensation all strategy for juniors is meaningless.*

1564

The Dark Side Of Golf. In the millions of golf books you'd be hard pressed to find one story about how golf ruined a man. There's just something about the *bright and alluring exterior* of golf that seems to prohibit any authenticity, or reference to dark interiors. Publishers and film producers are all ears when you have a golf comedy. If you have a tragedy, something that mirrors the star-crossed story of a man flaming out in the American Dream, we'll call you. Golf tragedy doesn't make any sense to the viewing or reading public. Golf tragedy would ruin the commercial value of any intellectual property---just as the following story may ruin the commercial value of this book.

Rod came to me with a proposition. He wanted me to fix his head for the Senior Tour, the early name for the Champions Tour. He was a plus one at Pumpkin Ridge. He had a loose, reliable swing. He knew he was a basket case. He still wanted to play on the Senior Tour. I asked him to get permission from his wife, and then we could get to work. He was a good putter under pressure and had a fine greenside touch. In his last amateur competition I was on the bag when he finished 3rd in the Trans-Mississippi held at Pumpkin's Witch Hollow course.

He started out in Arizona at senior winter events and posted some excellent numbers. His PGN was 68. A second, two thirds. He'd already established respect on the tee when he started listening to the circling vultures. The swing gurus that follow what was then called the Senior Tour like hoary hookers. "I fixed Jack's chipping grip." "I added twenty yards to Lee's drives." "Arnie and I fish together every winter" I couldn't be there, so I said, "Stick to your swing, it's the organic product of your entire athletic history. Stick to the strategy, it's working fine." Well, they got him more upright. They rotated his hand position at the top. They locked his legs. They switched his putter out. When the time came to tackle Monday qualifiers Rod was a wreck. He's shooting even par, he's shooting in the high 70s, then he can't break 80. I suggested he go home to his wife and two beautiful young daughters for a month or so, let everything wash over.

He couldn't do that. His wife was over the edge. He'd lied. She was violently opposed to the idea from the beginning. She's threatening everything. Now he doesn't know what to do. She's filing for divorce, he can't talk to his daughters. He's got a job at a driving range in Canada. He'll try for the Canadian Tour in the fall. Two years later I learn Rod was found dead in a trailer sixty miles north of Calgary. Attached to the trailer was a huge practice net facing south. It hit me hard. It should hit you hard. For every happy Hollywood ending in pro golf, there are a hundred trailer tragedies. And not just at the bottom. If Tiger can't overcome the dark side he'll end up in a Hollywood hotel overdosed on sleeping pills.

The dark side of golf. Nobody talks about it. Lives ruined, marriages crushed, minds cracked and missing in action. Empty slacks of castrated ambition ambling over to another lesson. Nobody wants to hear about it. Nobody wants to write about it. Nobody wants to read about it. So that's why it's here. I wasn't being facetious when I asked you to turn to your lady and ask the right question. *If you try to go it alone on tour golf will snap your spine.*

The Elusive And Essential Experience Of Good Contact. Winning golf demands good contact with your Self, Nature, and the ball. The best way to create good contact with your Self is to will a future winning Self. The force of your Will links the future to the present and the win becomes a natural extension of your being-here to your being-there.

Good contact with Nature means to understand the physicality of your being-here *at this specific course, on this specific day*. You feel the essential logic and lay of the land, you detect the changes of a morning breeze as it becomes a blustery afternoon wind, you deduce the speed of the greens at a glance. The more you identify with the course the more you can solve the tactical problems imbedded in the layout by the architect.

Good contact with the ball means to apply optimal swing mechanics *to this specific ball.* Your being-here is framed and focused by this white sphere on the grass. You *are* the ball and your job is to get into the hole as quickly as possible. Your stroke satisfies this desire. Good contact is more a seduction than a domination, more an intimate experience than a technical program. Contact with the ball is the most important form of good contact but competitive players court disaster if they neglect the other two. The history of the PGA Tour hangs heavy with the invisible asterisks of prodigious ball-strikers, who flamed out because they never knew *who or where they really were.*

The Shield. Pros carry the logo of their corporate sponsor on their bags. It takes a little sting out of the relentless tour anxiety. They start out being grateful for free sticks and the relationship cascades naturally forward until at some point they're brokering a few square inches on their shirt and cap for millions of dollars. Amateurs generally carry the logos of bag and club manufacturers. At the high school or collegiate level, competitive players are proud to display their school colors and mascots. It's a logical and public display of team unity, of the combat unit. The knight, however, *represents only himself.*

This is his favorite freedom, his hard-won autonomy. He eschews the corporate logo in favor of a family coat of arms that *distinguishes his personal presence* on the course. It can be the heraldry of animals, weapons and flowers. It can be the traditional colors of the clan. It can be rampant silver lions, dueling red and white dragons, rich designs of roses, crosses, and chessboards. The knight's shield proclaims his identity to every other competitor in the field. It says you will not be defeated by an anonymous sword, you will not be defeated by a corporate lackey, you will be defeated by *me*.

Ben Hogan despised golf pros wearing ads like streetwalkers with sandwich boards. On the PGA Tour today, a pro without a corporate logo on his cap is telling the world, "This Space For Sale." He's pimping himself. He longs to *sell his identity to the highest bidder* like his peers. The golf reform introduced in this book will announce itself to the sporting world when the first pros hang up these golden chains and compete behind their own personal shields. Then they'll be true knights, they'll be free, they'll reclaim American Golf from the hegemony of the lesser games. Once these colorful shields are seen by television viewers on the leaderboards, amateurs will understand the nihilism of the New Medieval, see the importance of their ancestry going forward and quickly follow suit.

The Grand Strategist. Throughout Old Medieval history one shield was prized above all others---the three black ravens of the Grand Strategist. If you took possession of this shield the battle was instantly won. Without rational coordination of military forces or the intelligence required to overcome disadvantageous terrain and numerically superior enemies there could be no victory. Only bloody chaos. Defeat. So the knight's strongest desire during battle was to *seize The Three Ravens at the first opportunity.*

Game Theory. The American mathematician John Von Neumann invented game theory in the 40s to describe the elusive behavior of economics. Since then it's been applied to many other fields, including biology, artificial intelligence and the stock market. The hypothesis of game theory is that individuals or groups follow a certain strategy---consciously or unconsciously---to optimize their chances of success. This theory can manifest itself in many ways, from a pretty girl putting on lipstick before a date to a professional baseball player warming up with a weighted bat. David Sklansky, in his 1987 groundbreaking book *Theory Of Poker*, introduced game theory strategies to poker. Instead of smoky anecdotes about fictional hands Sklansky's statistical analysis revealed the optimum style of play that generates the biggest monetary return. In one brilliant instance of mathematical insight, Sklansky proved you have to bluff every 11 hands to get paid off when you have the nuts. The global popularity of televised Texas Hold 'Em has spawned scores of new poker theories that have refined and extended Sklansky's original ideas.

A strong analog of my golf strategy is Edward O. Thorp's 1962 seminal work on casino blackjack *Beat The Dealer.* In poker you're playing against a number of other opponents and the psychological advantage of mental domination, emotional manipulation and 'doing the wrong thing at the right time' is immense. Non-stop, annoying conversation is a classic ploy in poker because a significant part of winning strategy is inducing your opponents to blunder when they bet, call, or raise. Blackjack is much closer to golf. In blackjack it's you against the house. In golf it's you against the course. If you spend time trying to produce bad play in your opponents the distraction ends up dismantling your own game.

Using an early IBM 704 computer at the MIT computation center, Thorp invented a blackjack theory that profoundly changed how the game was played by giving the edge to the player. His strategy was based on counting the cards. When the deck is favorable---rich with aces, tens and royalty---you raise the bet. When the deck is unfavorable you lower the bet or walk away. By monitoring the momentum of the most recent cards Thorp proved that a smart player beats the house. In my golf theory, by monitoring the momentum of your most recent holes, the smart golfer beats the course.

Thorp's blackjack theory was sophisticated by the mysterious Mr. M, who recruited a succession of MIT students to form professional blackjack teams starting in the late 70s. In the 90s intrepid incarnations of the MIT blackjack team won millions of dollars from casinos in Las Vegas, the Caribbean and Europe. The only way the house could prevent the loss of future millions was to bar the highly trained and intelligent teams playing Mr. M's signaling system. It took 30 years for Thorp's game theory to become universally known and today, after 49 years, his original blackjack theory remains the platform for all new variations.

When game theory is applied to a card game like blackjack the player's performance is primarily a matter of mental concentration. If the deck is plus 10 and you have 14 against the dealer's upturned 6 you stay because you know it's the correct play, even if you've been at the tables for 72 hours straight and you're falling off the stool. With golf the application of theory is more complex because it requires athletic prowess as well. It clearly takes far more physical ability to hit a golf ball a precise distance with the desired spin than scratch the felt of a table with your forefinger. A successful golf strategy has to unify mind and body, expectations with performance. If you practice with diligence and follow golf strategy with discipline you'll inevitably arrive at the point where *you hit a great shot before you actually decide which club to use.*

Naturally I'm pleased when players win tournaments using my strategy, even if the only competing strategies are 'Try to birdie every hole', or 'Try to get it back on this one.' Thorp's blackjack theory was used by gambling connoisseurs long before the MIT players extracted big money from the casinos and the subsequent press coverage brought public awareness. The most satisfying validation of a winning game theory, however, is when it wins at the highest level. Once my golf strategy helps a professional win on the PGA, the LPGA or European Tour there should be a small flurry of energizing critiques and improvements. Then, as it comes down to Playing The J against the Hanns variation on the last nine holes of the US Open, we'll finally have a serious discussion of *golf as a game*.

Queen Elizabeth II My extensive use of Old Medieval imagery to illustrate the New Medieval and the knight as metaphor for the true golfer finds a degree of corroboration in the decision of Queen Elizabeth II to confer knighthood on Nick Faldo. This dubbing of the first living English golfer was no royal caprice. With her customary genius for connecting with the British people Queen Elizabeth responded to the pillorying Nick received in the American sporting press after his losing tenure as British captain in the 2008 Ryder Cup. The caricature of the independent Faldo as arrogant and aloof struck a defensive cord in the hearts of British golfers. The Queen and her advisors were clearly listening to the din. A royal ceremony that for centuries had become tedious and hollow suddenly catches fire with prestige and meaning.

Nick Faldo may have lost the Ryder Cup, but he's won six majors and he's English to the core. He's our Nick, he's *our Sir Nick now.* The cultural significance of the knight's being-here is back. The Old Medieval is symbolically joined to the New, and the golfer has a major role onstage. Fortunately you don't have to wait for a call-back from the Queen. If you understand the central ideas of this book *you can knight yourself.* As you'll see shortly, all it takes is courage under fire and a little imagination.

In the Old Medieval only newly dubbed knights could wear a white belt. Look at all the white belts coming out in tournaments. Is this simply fashion, or does it reveal the deep physic identity of golfer and knight in the New Medieval?

The knight is a comedy mounted on a trajedy, his laughter the true independence.

The Burgess Society conducts its annual National Championships in three qualifying stages---local, regional and zonal. Winners of the four Zonals traditionally meet at Pacific Dunes at Bandon on the southern Oregon coast to decide National Champions in the six categories. As a matter of principle we don't award cash or trophies. The winners of each Burgess category are given the honorific "Victor" or "Victoria" for a year and Society members generally address them in this manner after their incumbencies, like American Presidents and Senators.

Pacific Dunes opened in 2001 and the top golf magazines soon ranked it #1 in America. It's a 6,633 yard links layout built into sand dunes on a cliff overlooking the Pacific Ocean. Architect Tom Doak drew Pacific Dunes as a stern test for professionals but wanted to keep it enjoyable for the average golfer. Because it's always blowing on the southern Oregon coast---from a one-club to a three-club wind depending on the season and the time of day---Tom took exceptional care with the short approaches to the greens. From fifty yards and in you have many options, and sometimes the best is using your putter.

You can't win without strategy here. When playing downwind Tom designed the holes without bunkers on one side of the fairway so you can run up your approach. If you're on the wrong side of a downwind hole the best play is often to pitch your ball to the correct side before attempting the green. Most of Tom's fairways feature treacherous pot bunkers. The large, sloped greens are protected by waste and blowout bunkers. You're playing from Oregon sand, but often your only visual reference is the Mauna Loa volcano on the big island of Hawaii. Because the track embodies the links philosophy of golf it can only be defeated by brains. The more you try to muscle your way to a score, the more Pacific Dunes will blow you away.

Respice · Finem

Rex won the Northwest Regional in the Snead class. He attended The Graduate School of Golf and plays a lot of Burgess events. Five-eleven, thinning sandy hair. Owns one of the largest independent real estate companies in the Northwest. Dresses and plays Nike. Was the handball champion at the Multnomah Athletic Club in 1999. No matter your business or profession, you know this man. He's the client from hell. He's always working an angle, a favor, a discount and no matter how well you treat him, you know there's a good chance he'll defect or stab you in the back. Whenever you help him he did it himself, and whenever he's too dense or obnoxious to learn it's your fault. His effusive, aggressive manner masks an envious, passive nature. So when Rex asks me to prep him for the Western Zonal in Palm Springs I naturally accept.

I'm especially alert for difficult conditions to test my strategy. When I don't *want* to do it. When the rapport is *rancid.* This type of opportunity arrives rarely, and I'm already thinking how to turn this dissonance into a Zonal win. I take him through a customized version of the strategic practice program, concentrating on the Three Points. These lessons are constantly interrupted by the inane ringtones of the two cell phones Rex carries on his belt like six-shooters. Talking to agents, talking to clients, talking to lenders. When we finally get to the fairway approaches a Hummer appears and Rex slips away, leaving behind a boisterous cloud of praise and a box of Macanudo cigars.

So of course Rex wins in Palm Springs and calls up drunk to compliment the timely utility of my strategy. He's got a proposition. Would I drop everything and prep him for the Burgess National Championships at Pacific Dunes? Would I caddy? I'm thinking there's no way in the world I'll play the squire to this particular fool when a notion breaks the glass jaw of my distaste---here's a chance to play a personal match with Tommy Armour. A little bet, a tight duel across fifty years. It's a clash of methods and confirmations. Can I carry Rex more than nine holes?

After poached chinook salmon at The Gallery Restaurant Rex and I talk finals strategy in the bar. He starts with flattery, saying how much his GSG education helped him win the Zonal at PGA West. He claims playing the Center Line and Three Points saved him at least ten strokes. He lights up the bar bragging about his putting stats---nine of nine two-footers and seven of eight six-footers. He shot 103 on the Nicklaus Course to win the Snead category by four. He confides *sotto voce* that his PGN is 110. So seven-under his ground score got him into the Championships. With the real estate industry in the tank Rex says he'd been too busy to play a practice round, so our hole mapping and tactical session concentrates primarily on ways to avoid Doak's punitive pot and blowout bunkers. With the ever-present wind and tournament pressure if all the competitors shoot in the Snead range the one who avoids the bunkers wins.

Rex concurs, but his eyes are already roving to the buxom blonde at the other end of the bar. With a PSN of 39 Rex has two strokes a hole and three extra strokes to make his personal pars. Over deep shots of bourbon we agree to take the extra strokes on holes 1, 7 and 13. In concert with Harvey Penick's advice that a player should continue to do what he usually does before a big round, I say nothing as Rex slowly fades to his right, drink and napkin in hand. Tomorrow he'll wake up in a strange bed. Hungover. Perfect. Having forgotten everything we'd planned. Perfect. *In my match with Tommy I want to be the underdog.*

As ample evidence that The Burgess Society doesn't always get it right, two of the finalists exercised the no-limit rule for the Championships. George won the Midwest. He's a mountain. At least six-six. Mid-fifties. Shaved head. Electrical engineer from Oklahoma City. He's got five putters, three chippers and four sand wedges---one a rusty track iron from the 1890s. His son Travis is on the bag. Six-eight all-state defensive end dressed in burgundy sweats.

Colt won the South. He's a wiry five-nine chiropractor from Miami. Late Thirties. Dark hair circling thick forearms. He's got two complete sets in his bag---a Ping and a Callaway. He's hired Freddy, the gaptoothed fellow we met earlier, the oldest caddy in the shack.

Anton won the North. Late-twenties. Long dark hair. He's a slender six-four video-game designer from Boston. Plays a standard set of Mizuno blades in a nylon bag. The kind pros put in the jumpseat of their Porsches for social rounds. A former Syracuse point guard with a rubber support on his left knee that squeaks when he walks.

So, George, Colt, Anton and Rex---the four Burgess Zonal winners hang fire around the first tee in disparate states of nervousness waiting to tee it up for the Burgess National Championships in the Snead Class. I'm standing about twenty yards away, admiring the expansive links landscape. The Pacific Ocean. The slow, tumbling swells. I've replaced the standard golf towel with a small white laundry bag. I'm ready. Like every championship final, a good start is essential. It's 10:15 in the morning.

The wind's already up---one club, maybe two. Rex is talking to Colt about the Portland real estate market. It's resisted the national crash well. Poised to rebound. There's tons of undervalued commercial out there. He's twisting his back. Do you know if there's a bench on the turn? Maybe one quick treatment could get me straight. Are you familiar with Reiki? He's talking to Anton about his bandage. Has he thought about acupuncture? Those needles kept him vertical for his handball trophy. He's talking to George about other electrical engineers from Oklahoma. Has he ever heard of R.A. Lafferty? Quite the Irish imagination. I think I saw in *Sports Illustrated* that your son's orally committed to Auburn. Or was it Texas Tech?

#1. 370 yards. Par-4. Uphill. Upwind. From the tee the fairway looks like a rumpled blanket to the clouds. You can't see the green. With a personal par of 7 Rex and I agreed last night that the proper play off the tee was a five-iron. After his fellow competitors hit drivers with the jackhammer urgency that normally accompanies first tee jitters Rex tees his ball and calls out,

"Driver!"

"What are we doing?"

"We're playing the first three holes for par. Gimme the driver!"

After seeing big George, little Colt, and athletic Anton all hit driver adrenaline quickly replaces the blood in Rex's brain. If they hit driver, he's hitting driver. With a truncated swing Rex skies his drive to the right. After five minutes of digging through the gorse and checking the lower limbs of pines George retreats to hit another shot from the tee. I'm holding out his utility wood. His competitors are hacking industrial up the fairway. The finalists for the Palmer class are watching the proceedings with studied reserve as they mentally count Rex's strokes.

"Gimme driver asshole!" Rex repeats his lurch and hits his second tee shot to the same area where we lost his first. He races to the area, quickly finds his ball and tops a seven-iron into a bunker guarding the right side of the fairway. Two tries to get out.

"Hit the wedge to your Second Point." So Rex tries for the green with a three iron that hangs in the wind and winds up in the left greenside bunker. He explodes over the green, chips long, lags from sixty feet and rattles in the uphill six-footer for 11.

AUXILIUM AB ALTO

#2. 368 yards. Par-4. Elevated tee. Upwind. Approaching the box Rex announces,

"This is ridiculous! An eleven? I quit! Where's the clubhouse from here? Gimme driver. OK, I'm playing for birdie in!" He's just seen his fellow competitors hit three knuckly drives into the wind.

"We're playing for par," I say, with as much neutrality as I can command, "your personal par was seven, so you're only four over. We're still playing for par."

"OK then, gimme driver." George, Colt and Anton are clearly embarrassed by our terse exchanges, trying to avoid eye contact, the contagion of strange behavior. One thing's perfectly clear, however. Any hidden or hovering resentment about the founder assisting a player in the National Championships has evaporated. The players are standing stonefaced, whispering to their caddies as I slowly walk up to Rex, snap his driver shaft over my knee and stash the pieces in the laundry bag. I don't say a word. What's to say? Nobody moves. Nobody even thinks about moving.

Rex is trying to erupt into profane indignities but nothing comes out and he accepts the 5-wood I put in his hands without protest. He skulls it to the center of the fairway just shy of a deep pot bunker. Hits a wedge to his Second Point. Hits the next fat and short of the green. Chips on. Two putts from twenty feet and he's in with 6. As we walk to the third tee Rex slows down, spins like he's going to ask directions and mug me in the alley but abruptly spins back and starts chatting amiably about changing out computer motherboards with George.

#3. 499 yards. Par-5. Upwind. Rex has the honor.

"We're still playing for par," I say, handing him a five-iron. He looks oddly at the club for a second, like it was the first time he'd ever seen such a thing in his life, then tees it up, takes a good turn and smacks the ball straight down the middle. The wind is swirling in unpredictable gusts. He punches another five-iron under the wind and over the pot bunkers to his Second Point. From there he hits a solid seven-iron that gets caught in a vortex, swings left, hits the front of the green and then slowly slips into a cavernous waste bunker. Something's happening now that merits attention. Rex is starting to play well under difficult conditions. With the pin on the back right, Rex has no visual reference and blasts over the green into the blowout bunker. He's slowing down, he's starting to use his brains. Instead of trying for the sucker pin with the tiny landing area he carves it out of the bunker sideways, leaving an eighty-foot putt. He reads it correctly, lags it tight and cans a two-footer for 7.

#4. 463 yards. Par-4. Downwind. Steep cliff along the right dropping to the beach. One of the most scenic and difficult holes on the course. His competitors hacked up the last hole so Rex has the honor again. He's joking with them at the box. Surveying the hole from behind the ball like the pros do on television.

"Driver!" Rex calls out, and all four players burst out laughing. Travis drops his dad's bag, he's laughing so hard. Rex waggles an imaginary club. He's turning his opponents into an audience. The first three monster holes are out of the way.

"No, check that, we're still playing for par. Hey Larry, make that another five-iron."

I hand him the five, thinking he's close to hysteria. He's not playing golf strategy, he's playing the words, the syntax of strategy. He's found a way to play *at* strategy. But his swing mechanics are in the groove. The lurch is gone, and Rex hits his tee shot crisply, low and left away from the cliff. After a bad bounce it winds up in the fairway waste bunker. From his position in the sand, all Rex can see is the powdery blue expanse of the sky and the navy stripe of the Pacific Ocean. To my astonishment he doesn't try to go for the green. He hits a simple sand wedge out of the bunker fifteen yards up the fairway. Hooding the face of his seven-iron he tries to hit his First Point just left of the green, but it takes a hard bounce and kicks over. A mediocre chip short, a good lag from thirty feet. Another two-footer and he's in with 6.

This makes three personal pars in a row. Rex is walking high on the tightrope, looking down at the crowd. He's jaunty, bubbly. A comedian on stage, a salesman on the lot. He's flying, but he's headed for a fall. The tightrope's getting tighter and his mind's starting to wobble.

#5. 199 yards. Par-3. Downwind. Rex still has the tee.

"I think I'll hazard a three-iron, please" he says in mock English accent to the amusement of everyone except Freddy. I hand him the club with the stage deference of a butler. It's all an act now. He shortens his swing, and tags it. It races towards the left side of the green, takes a lucky bounce and runs back to the flagstick fifteen feet away. After a good half hour watching the other players flail from one bunker to the next, Rex lips out his sidehill putt and taps in for 3. A personal eagle.

"Easy game." Rex annotates to the wide world.

#6. 316 yards. Par-4. Downwind.

"We're really playing for birdie now!" trumpets Rex, taking the 3-wood from the bag. I remind him he hasn't hit the 3, it's a short hole, he's been hitting his five-iron sweet. He shrugs, swings well and hits a hard pull that carries into the huge bunker protecting the left front of the green. He's twenty feet below the surface. Buried in a fried egg lie. After a mighty dig, he's still in the bunker, but now he can see the ball. His explosion screams out of the bunker, hits the pin and drops six feet away. After Anton sinks a thirty-footer, Rex steps up and knocks his putt in the heart. Two personal eagles in a row.

#7. 464 yards. Par 4. Downwind.

"Screw the strategy. We're playing for eagle now!" says Rex, waggling his 3-wood. He's been watching his opponents more closely. Counting their shots. Confident he's leading. This time his swing looks like a shelf of soup cans falling to the grocery floor. He hits the ground a foot behind the ball and chunks it into the waste area. After a drop he still has the 3 wood in his hand. His neck's turning beet red. I suggest the trusty five-iron, but he waves me off, takes a wild swing with the wood and tops it back into the waste. He drops another ball, barely clears the thick weeds with his next. Playing in a fog of dark energy Rex skulls another 3-wood, hits a wedge to the center of the green, and sinks a thirty-footer for an 8. He's digging fingernails into his left forearm, the blood's dripping slowly in two strands towards his wrist.

#8. 400 yards. Par-4. Upwind.

"We're playing for par," I say, extending the five-iron to Rex on the 8th tee. His hands are shaking but the bleeding has stopped. After the other players hit he stubbornly takes out the 3-wood, and manages to block it into the fairway. The wind is rising again, and shifting directions. At least two, maybe three clubs. Rex hits yet another 3-wood that looks spectacular, landing just in front of the green, saluting the pin and then disappearing into the back blowout bunker. Here, with the wind howling in everybody's ears, Rex slips into a loop of self-destruction He blasts out of the left bunker into the right bunker. Out of the right bunker over the green back into the left bunker. Back into the right bunker. Back into the left bunker. George and Travis refuse to watch. They're slowly cleaning their clubs at the side of the green. Colt's doing yoga on the back fringe. Anton's practicing his putting stroke beside his bag. Back into the right bunker. Rex finally finds the green with his eighth shot. It ends up four feet from the hole and he stubs it in for 9.

#9. 406 yards. Par-4. Downwind. Two greens. As we approach the upper tee Rex yells out,

"That's it! I quit! One of you bastards can win, I don't care. I quit!" I walk a half-step with him in the vague direction of the club house when I suddenly realize where we are. We've only finished *eight holes*. So I stop and let him get a few yards ahead.

"Victor Rex" I say, "call out your will. You're going to win today."

"My what?" answers Rex.

I take out his 3-wood, break the shaft over my knee, and put it in the laundry bag with the broken driver. Rex is storming up the incline to nail me.

"And this is for Tommy," I say, snapping his sand wedge shaft.

"Not the sand!".

He's at the lip of the tee box, leading with a big roundhouse right, when I duck and hit him with a short punch to the heart. Due to his precarious balance Rex flips in the air and falls hard on his back. He's unhorsed. Definitely unhorsed. For the wide world to see. He's up quickly, cursing, trying to mangle me but slips. He tries again. Slips again. Now the other men decide to intervene. They bunch up like NFL referees and keep us apart. After struggling against Travis Rex calms down. Way down. Scary down.

"Right, so now we're playing for par again." Rex says in monotone and hits a crisp five-iron straight down the middle. A hybrid to the fringe. A mediocre chip to the gigantic green, two putts from twenty feet and he's in with 5. That's a smooth 59 for the front nine. Colt shoots 55, George 52, and Anton 49. In this strong Oregon wind, with the drama vacillating between slapstick comedy and Greek tragedy the game's still on.

#10. 206 yards. Par-3. Before making the climb to the upper tee, both George and Colt lighten up for the back nine. Colt flips a coin and tells Freddy to drop his Callaways back at the clubhouse. George takes a 7-wood, a five-iron, a seven-iron, a sand wedge and a putter out of his bag and asks Travis to drop the other 25 clubs at the clubhouse. He's going to win with five clubs. He's going to win with style. Anton watches his opponents go through these adjustments with the nonchalance of an ex-athlete. His body language says he's got the win dialed in. His young face says he's got a lock against these old clowns. The Palmer finalists behind us are having a little trouble on #9 so there may be enough time for the caddies to make the trek to the clubhouse and back. Nobody mentions the punch. It hangs in the air like a collective conspiracy. Like an impending lawsuit. Like something that changes everything and simultaneously changes nothing. It wasn't part of the plan, but it happened, and now I carry a bag full of unknown consequences.

“Who’s Tommy?” asks Anton.
“We’re playing for birdie” I say to Rex, ignoring the question. Rex takes an aggressive line with his five-iron and hits his First Point twenty yards short and left of the green. A pitching wedge to five feet, and he makes the putt for 3, a personal hole-in-one. Wait! Rex walks over to Anton, his scorer. He says the ball moved while he was addressing his wedge.
“With the penalty stroke, mark me down for a 4 on this hole” says Rex loudly so the others can hear. This classic move is a major shock. George stares at Rex for over a minute, his big jaw hanging to the buttons on his shirt. Colt immediately starts organizing the bowels of his golf bag. Anton’s caught in a maze. With a single pencil stroke his lead is now in peril. Rex had been listening all along. It just took a blow at the right moment to activate his will. After being dehorsed Rex understood his true identity as a knight. He’s in full attack mode now.

#11. 148 yards. Par-3. Upwind.

"I believe we're still playing for birdie," says Rex cheerfully, sticking his tee into the ground with a twist. He takes a three-iron, executes a good turn and follow through. The ball hangs on a perfect low line and falls just short of the green.

"That's what I call good contact!" trumpets Rex as he stands to the side of the tee-box in a billiard pose, looking like a cat who's just swallowed a streetfull of condos. After a series of mediocre shots by his opponents, Rex chips up to fifteen feet, slides the first over the edge and makes the two-footer coming back for 4. Anton leaks his five-iron into the blowout bunker greenside right, then sends *six balls in a row* to Davy Jones' Locker. After some more thrashing Anton holes out for 17. It takes him three tries to get his ball out of the cup. On this gorgeous hole, Colt and George both lose their compass in the strong wind and eventually three-putt for double digit scores. Now Rex has all the momentum.

#12. 529 yards. Par-5. Upwind. With everything going his way Rex doesn't utter a word. He just smiles and smacks a 5-wood to the middle of the wide fairway. Plays a five-iron to the Center Line short of the main fairway bunkers, a seven-iron over the bunkers to his First Point, a safe wedge to twenty feet, and two putts for 6. This makes four straight personal birdies. George changes his mind, and asks Travis to go back to the clubhouse and get the rest of his clubs. His deep tactic simply isn't working. Colt's putting on Chapstick with the fixed and detached look of an embalmer. He's deep breathing as the four players stroll together up the flat fairway. Anton's walking with a noticeable limp, listening for noises from his left knee.

#13. 444 yards. Par-4. Upwind. A steep cliff runs along the left side. Rex marches to the tee and says,
"Well, it certainly looks like I'm playing for birdie again, maestro."
He comes over the top and snaps his 5-wood left. On the beach. As I'm reaching for the five-iron, he tees up another, and pull-hooks it west. On the beach. Declining to catch my eye, Rex pops up another 5-wood right and stomps up the fairway digging fingernails into his left arm. The blood starts to flow again.

George finds the fairway and Colt's hacking predictably up the safe right side. Anton's falling behind. His limp's getting worse, he's sitting on the ground. Rex goes over. He's calling the clubhouse on his cell. Anton's tossed in the towel, he's waiting for a cart to come out from the clubhouse. It looks like the time he got low-bridged driving to the hoop in the Villanova game and lost his senior season. Sitting on the bench, watching the time wind down on the clock. It's not the knee. With six holes to go in a two-club wind, he still has a chance. It's not the 17. Meanwhile George is playing the hole low and smart. Colt's still plugging along the right. Rex forgets his Points and plants another 5-wood in the deep right bunker.

"Damn your eyes Larry, you'll be hearing from my lawyer," he mutters, lamenting his missing sand wedge. He lays open his pitching wedge with a grimace. After two tries he's out and sinks a thirty-footer for 9.

#14. 145 yards. Par-3. Downwind. George has the honor with a fine 5. He's a big bald mountain on the tee waiting for Travis to show up with the rest of his clubs. He hits a safe seven-iron and finds the left front of the green. Colt hits into the deep blowout bunker right. With the wind at his back Rex pauses and says directly to me,

"This grip sure feels good!"

He hits a soft little nine-iron to his First Point short of the left bunker. An easy pitch to the green and two putts from twenty feet for 4.

#15. 539 yards. Par-5. Downwind. Travis arrives with the stuffed bag and George hits a jumbo driver long down the middle.

"Gimme driver. I'm playing for birdie!" says Rex, sarcastically. He slices his 5-wood right, almost loses another ball. Takes an unplayable lie, scuffs it in the dunes a few more times, finally reaches the fairway and skulls an approach over the green. Close to the gorse. He chips down the hill and makes a ten-footer for 8. Colt's wheels have finally come off. He's looking at the sky. Freddy's smoking a cigarette in his gap, making an obscene gesture.

It's not the tops. It's not the shanks. Colt simply disappears into his mind. He's back in his Miami office manipulating bad backs and sore shoulders. He's out with his young wife to The White Flamingo, their favorite nightclub. He can see the ice cubes rolling bourbon in the glass. He's laughing with his friends. He's got the story all worked out. This caddy punches this guy and then everything goes south. He can't focus on his game any more. Let's take the boat out tomorrow honey. Hey Mr. Boogie, you want to come along? He selects a small cloud and puts it in his trousers. Follows Freddy on the long walk to the clubhouse. So Anton's out. Colt's out. It's between Rex and a newly resurgent George for the Burgess National Championship.

#16. 338 yards. Par-4. Downwind. George belts another great drive headed for the green but it veers off into the deep hollow on the right. Rex steps up carefully to the tee box and says,

"Playing for par, har de har har."

For a second I think he's snapped. So much has gone down. He hits *pitching wedge* off the tee. Hits another wedge up the fairway to his Second Point, and a third wedge to the green. It backs up onto the fringe, but he has a relatively easy chip to ten feet and two putts for 6. Meanwhile George can't master the art of scaling a big greenside knob with proper pace. He tries a sand wedge, a seven-iron, and a 3-wood. They all take a peek at the green and roll agonizingly back to his feet. Now he tries a nine-iron. It flies the pin and catches the blowout bunker behind the green. It takes George two to get out. Three putts for 10.

#17. 208 yards. Par-3. Upwind. Rex throws up a few blades of grass and they immediately vanish. He figures he has George by two shots. The big bunker protecting the left is the primary danger. Rex hoods his pitching wedge and manages to land it close to his Second Point short of the bunkers. George gambles for the green with a 3-wood and plugs into the left bunker. Standing over his second shot, Rex suddenly becomes so nervous he wiffs it. He backs off, smiles, and hits a good third. It catches the lip of the same bunker and tumbles in, close to George's ball. Rex is away. He cuts it out with his pitching wedge and stands solemnly as George blasts out over the green and into the gorse. He can't find his ball so he has to play another from the bunker. It takes him three more swings to get out. George guns his putt. It rolls directly over the cup without deviating a dimple and ends up twenty feet away. Rex makes a tricky four-footer for 6 and George holes the long comebacker for 9. Unless Rex does something idiotic on the last he wins.

#18. 591 yards. Par-5. Downwind. Rex is five strokes up. He knows what to do. He hits a five-iron thin off the tee. Yanks his next five-iron into the waste bunker on the left, but calmly plays out sideways. Hits a wedge to his Second Point, and his fifth onto the green, about thirty feet from the cup. George is on the green in three, forty feet away. He three putts for 6. Rex leaves his first putt fifteen feet short, runs the second six feet past and misses the return. He finishes a marvelous putting day with a four-putt. Rex shoots 55 on the back, 114 for the round and wins the Snead Class by two shots.

"Excellent win Victor Rex," says George, giving him a friendly slap on the back, "especially after that rough start."

"I just know how to pick caddies," quips Rex as we all shake hands, and head up the path towards the bar. It's 4:15 in the afternoon

So I win my little match with Tommy and Victor Rex is Burgess National Champion. Tomorrow and tomorrow George, Colt and Anton will best remember the punch, the three broken clubs, and Rex hitting wedges off the tee, but it's crystal clear to me now that the defining moment occurred when Rex called the penalty stroke on himself at #10. I was close. Not only was Rex the only one to see his ball move---*the ball never actually moved.* In the heat of battle Rex invented a penalty on himself to gain the competitive edge. At the most unlikely moment, the client from hell discovers his true identity as a knight and goes on to win the tournament with a masterpiece of golf strategy.

When asked of his greatest day in golf Bobby Jones said it was a small match played at the National Golf Links in Southampton when he shot 73 in a gale. That round in difficult conditions gave him more happiness and satisfaction than any of his more famous, major-winning efforts. Since I started my first golf school in LA I've seen a lot of the luminous side of golf and a few heavy doses of the dark side as well. The Snead Class Championships at Pacific Dunes was a whirlwind of reality and hyper-reality, a violent and unpredictible confirmation of method even by theatrical or literary standards. The Johns Golf Strategy was ignored, forgotten, recovered, cursed, imposed by force, forgotten again, mocked, and then mysteriously refined to achieve the win.

It was my greatest day in golf because the strategy worked for the player *and for the man.* Rex grew a third testicle, he willed to will more, he freed himself. No teacher can ask more than this. So as the sun goes down on the southern Oregon coast, splashing the horizon with interlocked orange and magenta, I welcome a proud kind of happiness as I raise a glass to Victor Rex and a second to Tommy Armour, the great teaching pro who got the idea of golf strategy rolling.

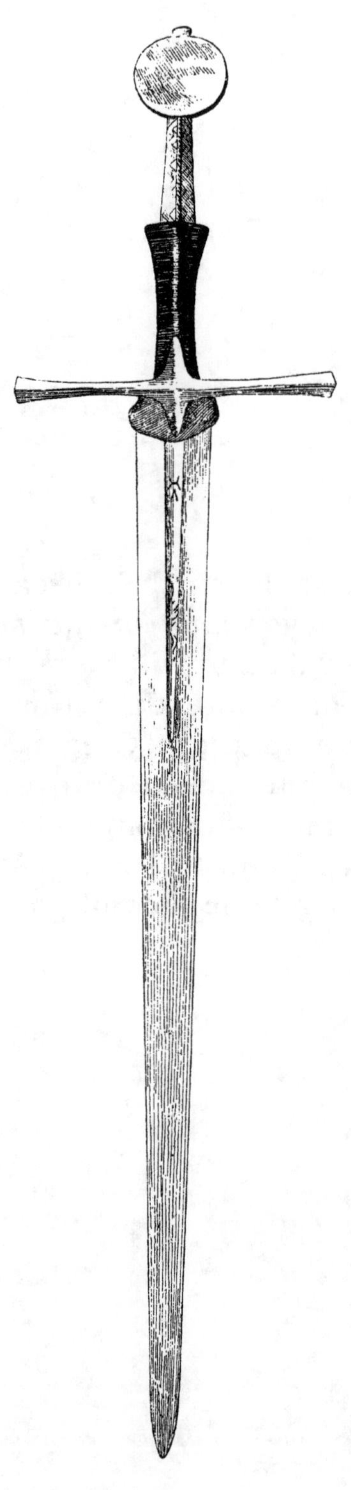

The Future Of Tiger Woods

Tiger Woods has hit the ball deeper into the rough than any golfer in history, he's entered the critical moment of self-doubt in the hero's journey. The desert. The bizarre temptations. The self-loathing, self-pity and self-deception. The most famous athlete in the world has been exposed as a fool playing *at* love and the most dangerous dragons have been witnessed breeding within his own psyche. Translating golf strategy into life strategy Tiger needs to play for par, wait for the momentum to swing his way before making a big move. He'll certainly return to winning tournaments and majors but his little rebellions and vignettes in the land of red lights have brutally and publicly exposed the fragility of his personal identity. As Nietzsche noted, rebellion is the characteristic of the slave.

To reaffirm the quest Tiger must will to become a knight, after disgrace and divorce. Seen through the lens of New Medieval conditioning it's clear that at no time in his life has Tiger actually been free. Not as a child prodigy, not as a teenager, not as a celebrity athlete or corporate trustee. Eldridge the boy prodigy was left to mature in confusion while the myth of Tiger was being packaged and distributed. First by his father and then by IMG. If he can't learn from his mistakes his way, if he allows the internal recalibration and personal meaning of his fall to be effected by corporate handlers Tiger will remain in chains, a single mistake from collapse. To fulfill his destiny as history's greatest golfer Tiger needs to create a true individuality independent of the Tiger mask and Tiger logo.

Bobby Jones showed the way. Rex the real estate broker confirmed it. To regain the strategic initiative with his fans and fellow competitors on the PGA Tour Tiger needs to call a penalty on himself for something that nobody has seen, for a violation that never occurred. This move could come *on or off* the course and will give him the time and space he needs to attack Nicklaus' record of 18 major wins with refreshed relentlessness.

As Tiger gets the next phase of his heroic narrative into high gear he must continue to watch and learn from the shadows of three men. After defeating Boris Spassky in a match during the heat of the Cold War for the world chess championship in 1971, Bobby Fischer became the American sports hero of the moment. After a brief victory lap he quickly fell off the board, joined a religious cult in Pasadena and ended up shuffling around the world for forty years as a ghostly shell of his former identity. Bobby died in Iceland, the site of his greatest victory, a crazy and embittered recluse.

Stu Unger was the best gin rummy player in history and won the World Series of Poker three times. He won millions of dollars multiple times and blew it all on sports gambling and crack cocaine. The drug made his nose look like a broken faucet and his life a dripping handout. Stu died in a cheap Las Vegas motel room with hookers going through the pockets of his corpse for stray bills.

Michael Jackson. The most dangerous shadow of the three. A child prodigy who became the King of Pop and the most famous entertainer in the world. Michael died in Los Angeles because he couldn't sleep. Anywhere.

The Future Of American Golf. The New Medieval will last 400 years and repeat the theological character of the Old Medieval. Mass conditioning generated by new perspective-shattering technologies will make this epoch feel longer than twelve generations. We'll experience the New Medieval as the forever condition, the eternal landscape of our speculations, the way things always were. Faith-based Will to Power will lock America down. The lesser games of war, politics, and economics will thrive by imitating the behavior and propaganda of the ruling religious apparatus. These games will introduce new laws, new slogans, new consensus standards, and merge their most immediate goals with the dogmas of the dominant faith. In this powerful and perplexing phase-shift of Western Civilization, in this security futurc that mimics thc past, a paradoxical drivc towards individuality will arise. The oppressive conformity of belief and the statistical simulations of public life will be overcome by the talent of great individuals. The dulling ideologies of marketplace, state and church will be countered by the pragmatic intelligence of the American family.

We'll witness the birth of a new American aristocracy, a cultural force only sporadically in fashion since the astounding first days of the American republic. The true knight will become the symbol of personal freedom and high ethics, the most celebrated face of American society. His chivalry will bring women back to men, his courage will bring men back to brotherhood.

In the dark military smoke, in the glittering philosophical mirrors, in the treacherous fundamentalist soil and endemic poverty of the New Medieval a new romanticism will bloom. Cruelty and intolerance will bring lovers together with ever more delicate and intimate oaths of affection. Being-here will come to mean being-in-love. In the jolt and rush, in the blasting sands and pounding waves of this high strangeness American Golf will adopt the optimal strategy to save her lovers and herself.

She'll be cautious, she'll play for par. She'll send out champions to secure world peace so she can attend to serious domestic problems. Initially she'll stop building new golf courses. As corporations fall further away from the halls of real power she'll restructure professional golf. She'll minimize the LPGA Tour, calendar fewer PGA Tour events, with less prize money and more restrictions on foreign pros. To compensate for these adjustments, she'll devote more time and resources to amateur golf. Backed by the patronage of the new aristocrats local, state and national amateur tournaments will enjoy unprecedented prestige and popularity. In 30 years the LPGA Tour will be gone, the PGA Tour down 60% and in 50 years the two most important golf tournaments in the world will once again be the British Amateur and the US Amateur. 200 years into the New Medieval 90% of urban golf courses will be converted to government housing, 90% of suburban and resort courses will be converted to critical commercial uses. Professional golf will lose its being-here and become a legend, a story of heroes and prodigious shots recounted in the dialects of awe beside a humble fire. Amateur golf will once again be kept safe as the ward of a small number of clubs and secret societies with sufficient power to protect her from the slings and arrows of the ruling priesthood.

From the false time and cramped space of the New Medieval one reassuring truth calls out to all golf lovers---American Golf will survive this long hegemony by staying true to herself. Golf is the greatest game and will continue to be the greatest game no matter how totalitarian, absurd or infantile the lesser games that attempt to define and drive American reality become. She'll be our green patch of reason in the technological madness, she'll be the dose of the Old Medieval that eventually cures us of the New. Yes, she will be noticeably slimmer. Yes, she may be wiser, but she'll still be your infinite lover.

She'll always know how to please a true knight.

Contacts

consciouspublishing.com

burgesssociety.com

graduateschoolofgolf.com

www.ingramcontent.com/pod-product-compliance
Lightning Source LLC
Chambersburg PA
CBHW060607310726
48982CB00008B/1261/J
* 9 7 8 1 9 2 9 0 9 6 1 0 7 *